# Evered

Ben Ames Williams

Alpha Editions

This edition published in 2021

ISBN : 9789355113986

Design and Setting By
**Alpha Editions**
www.alphaedis.com
Email - info@alphaedis.com

As per information held with us this book is in Public Domain.
This book is a reproduction of an important historical work. Alpha Editions
uses the best technology to reproduce historical work in the same manner
it was first published to preserve its original nature. Any marks or number
seen are left intentionally to preserve its true form.

# Contents

| | |
|---|---|
| CHAPTER I | - 1 - |
| CHAPTER II | - 5 - |
| CHAPTER III | - 11 - |
| CHAPTER IV | - 17 - |
| CHAPTER V | - 20 - |
| CHAPTER VI | - 25 - |
| CHAPTER VII | - 31 - |
| CHAPTER VIII | - 36 - |
| CHAPTER IX | - 40 - |
| CHAPTER X | - 44 - |
| CHAPTER XI | - 49 - |
| CHAPTER XII | - 53 - |
| CHAPTER XIII | - 61 - |
| CHAPTER XIV | - 63 - |
| CHAPTER XV | - 69 - |
| CHAPTER XVI | - 75 - |
| CHAPTER XVII | - 81 - |
| CHAPTER XVIII | - 88 - |
| CHAPTER XIX | - 94 - |

# CHAPTER I

THERE is romance in the very look of the land of which I write. Beauty beyond belief, of a sort to make your breath come more quickly; and drama—comedy or tragedy according to the eye and the mood of the seer. Loneliness and comradeship, peace and conflict, friendship and enmity, gayety and somberness, laughter and tears. The bold hills, little cousins to the mountains, crowd close round each village; the clear brooks thread wood and meadow; the birches and scrub hardwood are taking back the abandoned farms. When the sun drops low in the west there is a strange and moving purple tinge upon the slopes; and the shadows are as blue as blue can be. When the sun is high there is a greenery about this northern land which is almost tropical in its richness and variety.

The little villages lie for the most part in sheltered valley spots. Not all of them. Liberty, for example, climbs up along a steep hill road on your way to St. George's Pond, or over the Sheepscot Ridge, for trout. No spot lovelier anywhere. But you will come upon other little house clusters, a white church steeple topping every one, at unsuspected crossroads, with some meadowland round and about, and a brook running through the village itself, and perhaps a mill sprawled busily across the brook. It is natural that the villages should thus seek shelter; for when the winter snows come down this is a harsh land, and bitter cold. So is it all the more strange that the outlying farms are so often set high upon the hills, bare to the bleak gales. And the roads, too, like to seek and keep the heights. From Fraternity itself, for example, there is a ten-mile ridge southwest to Union, and a road along the whole length of the ridge's crest, from which you may look for miles on either side.

This is not a land of bold emprises; neither is it one of those localities which are said to be happy because they have no history. There is history in the very names of the villages hereabouts. Liberty, and Union, and Freedom; Equality, and Fraternity. And men will tell you how their fathers' fathers came here in the train of General Knox, when that warrior, for Revolutionary services rendered, was given title to all the countryside; and how he sub-granted to his followers; and how they cleared farms, and tilled the soil, and lumbered out the forests, and exterminated deer and moose and bear. Seventy years ago, they will tell you, there was no big game hereabouts; but since then many farms, deserted, have been overrun by the forests; and the bear are coming back, and there are deer tracks along every stream, and moose in the swamps, and wildcats scream in the night. Twenty or thirty or forty miles to the north the big woods of Maine begin; so that this land is an outpost of the wilderness, thrust southward among the closer dwellings of man.

The people of these towns are of ancient stock. The grandfathers of many of them came in with General Knox; most of them have been here for fifty years or more, they or their forbears. A few Frenchmen have drifted down from Quebec; a few Scotch and Irish have come in here as they come everywhere. Half a dozen British seamen escaped, once upon a time, from a man-of-war in Penobscot Bay, and fled inland, and were hidden away until their ship was gone. Whereupon they married and became part and parcel of the land, and their stock survives. By the mere reading of the names of these folk upon the R. F. D. boxes at their doors you may know their antecedents. Bubier and Saladine, Varney and Motley, McCorrison and MacLure, Thomas and Davis, Sohier and Brine—a five-breed blend of French and English, Scotch and Welsh and Irish; in short, as clear a strain of good Yankee blood as you are like to come upon.

Sturdy folk, and hardy workers. You will find few idlers; and by the same token you will find few slavish toilers, lacking soul to whip a trout brook now and then or shoot a woodcock or a deer. Most men hereabouts would rather catch a trout than plant a potato; most men would rather shoot a partridge than cut a cord of wood. And they act upon their inclinations in these matters. The result is that the farms are perhaps a thought neglected; and no one is very rich in worldly goods; and a man who inherits a thousand dollars has come into money. Yet have they all that any man wisely may desire; for they have food and drink and shelter, and good comradeship, and the woods to take their sport in, and what books they choose to read, and time for solid thinking, and beauty ever before their eyes. Whether you envy or scorn them is in some measure an acid test of your own soul. Best hesitate before deciding.

Gregarious folk, these, like most people who dwell much alone. So there are grange halls here and there; and the churches are white-painted and in good repair; and now and then along the roads you will come to a picnic grove or a dancing pavilion, set far from any town. Save in haymaking time the men work solitary in the fields; but in the evening, when cows have been milked and pigs fed and wood prepared against the morning, they take their lanterns and tramp or drive half a mile or twice as far, and drop in at Will Bissell's store for the mail and for an hour round Will's stove.

You will hear tales there, tales worth the hearing, and on the whole surprisingly true. There is some talk of the price of hay or of feed or of apples; but there is more likely to be some story of the woods—of a bull moose seen along the Liberty road or a buck deer in Luke Hills' pasture or a big catch of trout in the Ruffingham Meadow streams. Now and then, just about mail time in the evening, fishermen will stop at the store to weigh their catches; and then everyone crowds round to see and remark upon the matter.

The store is a clearing-house for local news; and this must be so, for there is no newspaper in Fraternity. Whatever has happened within a six-mile radius during the day is fairly sure to be told there before Will locks up for the night; and there is always something happening in Fraternity. In which respect it is very much like certain villages of a larger growth, and better advertised.

There is about the intimacy of life in a little village something that suggests the intimacy of life upon the sea. There is not the primitive social organization; the captain as lord of all he surveys. But there is the same close rubbing of shoulders, the same nakedness of impulse and passion and longing and sorrow and desire. You may know your neighbor well enough in the city, but before you lend him money, take him for a camping trip in the woods or go with him to sea. Thereafter you will know the man inside and out; and you may, if you choose, make your loan with a knowledge of what you are about. It is hard to keep a secret in a little village; and Fraternity is a little village—that and nothing more.

On weekday nights, as has been said, Will Bissell's store is the social center of Fraternity. Men begin to gather soon after supper; they begin to leave when the stage has come up from Union with the mail. For Will's store is post office as well as market-place. The honeycomb of mail boxes occupies a place just inside the door, next to the candy counter. Will knows his business. A man less wise might put his candies back among the farming tools, and his tobacco and pipes and cigars in the north wing, with the ginghams, but Will puts them by the mail boxes, because everyone gets mail or hopes for it, and anyone may be moved to buy a bit of candy while he waits for the mail to come.

This was an evening in early June. Will's stove had not been lighted for two weeks or more; but to-night there was for the first time the warm breath of summer in the air. So those who usually clustered inside were outside now, upon the high flight of steps which led up from the road. Perhaps a dozen men, a dog or two, half a dozen boys. Luke Hills had just come and gone with the season's best catch of trout—ten of them; and when they were laid head to tail they covered the length of a ten-foot board. The men spoke of these trout now, and Judd, who was no fisherman, suggested that Luke must have snared them; and Jim Saladine, the best deer hunter in Fraternity and a fair and square man, told Judd he was witless and unfair. Judd protested, grinning meanly; and Jean Bubier, the Frenchman from the head of the pond, laughed and exclaimed: "Now you, m'sieu', you could never snare those trout if you come upon them in the road, eh?"

They were laughing in their slow dry way at Judd's discomfiture when the hoofs of a horse sounded on the bridge below the store; and every man looked that way.

It was Lee Motley who said, "It's Evered."

The effect was curious. The men no longer laughed. They sat quite still, as though under a half-fearful restraint, and pretended not to see the man who was approaching.

## CHAPTER II

THERE were two men in the buggy which came up the little ascent from the bridge and stopped before the store. The men were Evered, and Evered's son, John. Evered lived on a farm that overlooked the Whitcher Swamp on the farther side. He was a man of some property, a successful farmer. He was also a butcher; and his services were called in at hog-killing time as regularly as the services of Doctor Crapo in times of sickness. He knew his trade; and he knew the anatomy of a steer or a calf or a sheep as well as Doctor Crapo knew the anatomy of a man. He was an efficient man; a brutally efficient man. His orchard was regularly trimmed and grafted and sprayed; his hay was re-seeded year by year; his garden never knew the blight of weeds; his house was clean, in good repair, white-painted. A man in whom dwelt power and strength; and a man whom other men disliked and feared.

He was a short man, broad of shoulder, with a thick neck and a square, well-shaped head, a heavy brow and a steady burning eye. A somber man, he never laughed; never was known to laugh. There was a blighting something in his gaze which discouraged laughter in others. He was known to have a fierce and ruthless temper; in short, a fearsome man, hard to understand. He puzzled his neighbors and baffled them; they let him well alone.

He was driving this evening. His horse, like everything which was his, was well-groomed and in perfect condition. It pranced a little as it came up to the store, not from high spirits, but from nervousness. So much might be known by the white glint of its eye. The nervousness of a mettled creature too much restrained. It pranced a little, and Evered's hand tightened on the rein so harshly that the horse's lower jaw was pulled far back against its neck, and the creature was abruptly still, trembling, and sweating faintly for no cause at all. Evered paid no more heed to the horse. He looked toward the group of men upon the steps, and some met his eye, and some looked away.

He looked at them, one by one; and he asked Lee Motley: "Is the mail come?"

Motley shook his head. He was a farmer of means, a strong man, moved by no fear of Evered. "No," he said.

Evered passed the reins to his son. "Hold him still," he told the young man, and stepped out over the wheel to the ground, dropping lightly as a cat. The horse gave a half leap forward and was caught by John Evered's steady hand; and the young man spoke gently to the beast to quiet it.

Evered from the ground looked up at his son and said harshly, "I bade you hold him still."

The other answered, "I will."

"You'd best," said Evered, and turned and strode up the steps into the store.

The incident had brought out vividly enough the difference between Evered and his son. They were two characters sharply contrasting; for where Evered was harsh, John was gentle of speech; and where Evered was abrupt, John was slow; and where Evered's eye was hard and angry, John's was mild. They contrasted physically. The son was tall, well-formed and fair; the father was short, almost squat in his broad strength, and black of hair and eye. Nevertheless, it was plain to the seeing eye that there was strength in John as there was strength in Evered—strength of body and soul.

When Evered had gone into the store Motley said to the son, "It's warm."

The young man nodded in a wistfully friendly way. "Yes," he agreed. "So warm it's brought up our peas this day."

"That south slope of yours is good garden land," Motley told him, and John said:

"Yes. As good as I ever see."

Everyone liked John Evered; and someone asked now: "Been fishing any, over at Wilson's?"

John shook his head. "Too busy," he explained. "But I hear how they're catching some good strings there."

"Luke Hills brought in ten to-night that was ten feet long," Jim Saladine offered. "Got 'em at Ruffingham."

The young man in the buggy smiled delightedly, his eyes shining. "Golly, what a catch!" he exclaimed.

Then Evered came to the door of the store and looked out, and silence fell upon them all once more. The mail was coming down the hill; the stage, a rattling, rusted, do-or-die automobile of ancient vintage, squeaked to a shrill stop before the very nose of Evered's horse. John spoke to the horse, and it was still. The stage driver took the mail sacks in, and Evered left the doorway. The others all got up and turned toward the door.

Motley said to Saladine, "Did you mark the horse? It was scared of the stage, but it was still at his word, and he did not tighten rein."

"I saw," Saladine agreed. "The boy handles it fine."

"It's feared of Evered; but the beast loves the boy."

"There's others in that same way o' thinking," said Saladine.

Inside the store Will Bissell and Andy Wattles, his lank and loyal clerk, were stamping and sorting the mail. No great matter, for few letters come to Fraternity. While this was under way Evered gathered up the purchases he had made since he came into the store, and took them out and stowed them under the seat of the buggy. He did not speak to his son. John sat still in his place, moving his feet out of the other's way. When the bundles were all bestowed Evered went back up the steps and Will gave him his daily paper and a letter addressed to his wife, and Evered took them without thanks, and left the store without farewell to any man, and climbed into the buggy and took the reins. He turned the horse sharply and they moved down the hill, and the bridge sounded for a moment beneath their passing. In the still evening air the pound of the horse's hoofs and the light whirring of the wheels persisted for long moments before they died down to blend with the hum and murmur of tiny sounds that filled the whispering dusk.

As they drove away one or two men came to the door to watch them go; and Judd, a man with a singular capacity for mean and tawdry malice, said loudly, "That boy'll break Evered, some day, across his knee."

There was a moment's silence; then Jean Bubier said cheerfully that he would like to see the thing done. "But that Evered, he is one leetle fighter," he reminded Judd.

Judd laughed unpleasantly and said Evered had the town bluffed. "That's all he is," he told them. "A black scowl and some cussing. Nothing else. You'll see."

Motley shook his head soberly. "Evered's no bluff," he said. "You're forgetting that matter of the knife, Judd."

Motley's reminder put a momentary silence upon them all. The story of the knife was well enough known; the knife they had all seen. The thing had happened fifteen or twenty years before, and was one of the tales many times told about Will's stove. One Dave Riggs, drunken and worthless, farming in a small way in North Fraternity, sent for Evered to kill a pig. Evered went to Riggs' farm. Riggs had been drinking; he was quarrelsome; he sought to interfere with Evered's procedure. Motley, a neighbor of Riggs, had been there at the time, and used to tell the story.

"Riggs wanted him to tie up the pig," he would explain. "You know Evered does not do that. He says they will not bleed properly, tied. He did not argue with the man, but Riggs persisted in his drunken way, and cursed Evered to his face, till I could see the blood mounting in the butcher's cheeks. He is a bad-tempered man, always was.

"He turned on Riggs and told the man to hush; and Riggs damned him. Evered knocked him flat with a single fist stroke; and while Riggs was still on the ground Evered turned and got the pig by the ears and slipped the knife into its throat, in that smooth way he has. When he drew it out the blood came after; and Evered turned to Riggs, just getting on his feet.

"'There's your pig,' said Evered. 'Butchered right. Now, man, be still.'

"Well, Riggs took a look at the pig and another at Evered. He was standing by the chopping block, and his hand fell on the ax stuck there. Before I could stir he had lifted it, whirling it, and was sweeping down on Evered.

"It was all over quick, you'll mind. Riggs rushing, with the ax whistling in the air. Then Evered stepped inside its swing, and drove at Riggs' head. I think he forgot he had the knife in his hand. But it was there; his hand drove it with the cunning that it knew—at the forehead of the other man.

"I mind how Riggs looked, after he had dropped. On his back he was, the knife sticking straight up from his head. And it still smeared with the pig's blood, dripping down on the dead man's face. Oh, aye, he was dead. Dead as the pig, when it quit its walking round in a little, and laid down, and stopped its squeal."

Someone asked him once, when he had told the tale: "Where was Riggs' wife? Married, wa'n't he?"

"In the house," said Motley. "The boy was there, though. He'd come to see the pig stuck, and when he saw the blood come out of its throat he yelled and run. So he didn't have to see the rest—the knife in his father's head."

There had been no prosecution of Evered for that ancient tragedy. Motley's story was clear enough; it had been self-defense at the worst, and half accident besides. Riggs' wife went away and took her son, and Fraternity knew them no more.

They conned over this ancient tale of Evered in Will's store that night; and some blamed him, and some found him not to blame. And when they were done with that story they told others; how when he was called to butcher sheep he had a trick of breaking their necks across his knee with a twist and a jerk of his hands. There was no doubt of the man's strength nor of his temper.

A West Fraternity man came in while they were talking; one Zeke Pitkin, a mild man, and timid. He listened to their words, and asked at last, "Evered?"

They nodded; and Pitkin laughed in an awkward way. "He killed my bull to-day," he said.

Will Bissell asked quickly, "Killed your bull? You have him do it?"

Pitkin nodded, gulping at his Adam's apple. "Getting ugly, the bull was," he said. "I didn't like to handle him. Decided to beef him. So I sent for Evered, and he came over."

He looked round at them, laughed uneasily. "He scared me," he said.

Motley asked slowly. "What happened, Zeke?"

Pitkin rubbed one hand nervously along his leg. "We-ell," he explained. "I'm nervous like. Git excited easy. So when he come I told him the bull was ugly. Told him to look out for it.

"He just only looked at me in that hard way of his. I had the bull in the barn; and he went in where it was and fetched it out in the barn floor. Left the bull standing there and begun to fix his tackle to h'ist it up.

"I didn't want to stay in there with the bull. I was scared of it—it loose there, nothing to hold it. And Evered kept working round it, back to the beast half the time. Nothing to stop it tossing him. I didn't like to get out, but I didn't want to stay. And I guess I talked too much. Kept telling him to hurry, and asking him why he didn't kill it and all. Got him mad, I guess."

The man shivered a little, his eyes dim with the memory of the moment. He took off his hat and rubbed his hand across his head, and Motley said, "He did kill it?"

Pitkin nodded uneasily. "Yeah," he said. "Evered turned round to me by and by; and he looked at me under them black eyebrows of his, and he says: 'Want I should kill this bull, do you?' I 'lows that I did. 'Want him killed now, do you?' he says, and I told him I did. And I did too. I was scared of that bull, I say. But not the way he did kill it."

He shuddered openly; and Motley asked again, "What did he do?"

"Stepped up aside the bull," said Pitkin hurriedly. "Yanked out that knife of his—that same knife—out of his sheath. Up with it, and down, so quick I never see what he did. Down with the knife right behind the bull's horns. Right into the neck bone. And that bull o' mine went down like a ton o' brick. Like two ton o' brick. Stone dead."

Will Bissell echoed, "Stabbed it in the neck?"

"Right through the neck bone. With that damned heavy knife o' his." He wiped his forehead again. "We had a hell of a time h'isting that bull, too," he said weakly. "A hell of a time."

No one spoke for a moment. They were digesting this tale of Evered. Then Judd said: "I'd like to see that red bull of his git after that man."

One or two nodded, caught themselves, looked sheepishly round to discover whether they had been seen. Evered's red bull was as well and unfavorably known as the man himself. A huge brute, shoulder high to a tall man, ugly of disposition, forever bellowing challenges across the hills from Evered's barn, frightening womenfolk in their homes a mile away. A creature of terror, ruthlessly curbed and goaded by Evered. It was known that the butcher took delight in mastering the bull, torturing the beast with ingenious twists of the nose ring, with blows on the leg joints, and nose, and the knobs where horns should have been. The red bull was of a hornless breed. The great head of it was like a buffalo's head, like a huge malicious battering ram. It was impossible to look at the beast without a tremor of alarm.

"It's ugly business to see Evered handle that bull," Will Belter said, half to himself.

And after a little silence Jean Bubier echoed: "Almost as ugly as to see the man with his wife. When I have see that, sometime, I have think I might take his own knife to him."

Judd, the malicious, laughed in an ugly way; and he said, "Guess Evered would treat her worse if he got an eye on her and that man Semler."

It was Jim Saladine's steady voice which put an end to that. "Don't put your foul mouth on her, Judd," he said quietly. "Not if you want to walk home."

Judd started to speak, caught Saladine's quiet eye and was abruptly still.

# CHAPTER III

EVERED and his son drove home together through the clotting dusk in a silence that was habitual with them. The buggy was a light vehicle, the horse was swift and powerful, and they made good time. Evered, driving, used the whip now and then; and at each red-hot touch of the light lash the horse leaped like a stricken thing; and at each whiplash John Evered's lips pressed firmly each against the other, as though to hold back the word he would have said. No good in speaking, he knew. It would only rouse the lightly slumbering anger in his father, only lead to more hurts for the horse, and a black scowl or an oath to himself. There were times when John Evered longed to put his strength against his father's; when he was hungry for the feel of flesh beneath his smashing fists. But these moments were few. He understood the older man; there was a blood sympathy between them. He knew his father's heart as no other did or could; and in the last analysis he loved his father loyally. Thus had he learned long patience and restraint. It is very easy to damn and hate a man like Evered, hot and fierce and ruthlessly overbearing. But John Evered, his son, who had suffered more from Evered than any other man, neither damned nor hated him.

They drove home together in silence. Evered sat still in his seat, but there was no relaxation in his attitude. He was still as a tiger is still before the charge and the leap. John at his side could feel the other's shoulder muscles tensing. His father was always so, always a boiling vessel of emotions. You might call him a powerful man, a masterful man. John Evered knew him for a slave, for the slave of his own hot and angry pulse beats. And he loved and pitied him.

Out of Fraternity they took the Liberty road, and came presently to a turning which led them to the right, and so to the way to Evered's farm, a narrow road, leading nowhere except into the farmyard, and traveled by few men who had no business there.

When they came into the farmyard it was almost dark. Yet there was still light enough to see, beyond the shadow of the barn, the sloping hillside that led down to Whitcher Swamp; and the swamp itself, brooding beneath its gray mists in the thickening night. The farm buildings were set on a jutting shoulder of the hill, looking out across the valley where the swamp lay, to Fraternity, and off toward Moody Mountain beyond the town. By day there was a glory in this valley that was spread below them; by night it was a place of dark and mystery. Sounds used to come up the hill from the swamp; the sounds of thrashing brush where the moose fed, or perhaps the clash of ponderous antlers in the fall, or the wicked scream of a marauding cat, or the harsh cries of night-hawks, or the tremolo hoot of an owl.

Built against the barn on the side away from the house there was a stout roofed stall; and opening from this stall a pen with board walls higher than a man's head and cedar posts as thick as a man's leg, set every four feet to support the planking of the walls. As the horse stopped in the farmyard and Evered and his son alighted, a sound came from this stall—a low, inhuman, monstrous sound, like the rumbling of a storm, like the complaint of a hungry beast, like the promise of evil things too dreadful for describing; the muffled roaring of Evered's great red bull, disturbed by the sound of the horse. John Evered stood still for an instant, listening. It was impossible for most men to hear that sound without an appalling tremor of the heart. But Evered himself gave no heed to it. He spoke to the horse. He said "Hush, now. Still."

The horse was as still as stone, yet it trembled as it had trembled at Will's store. Evered gathered parcels from beneath the seat; and John filled his arms with what remained. They turned toward the house together, the son a little behind the father.

There was a light in the kitchen of the farmhouse; and a woman had come to the open door and was looking out toward them. She was silhouetted blackly by the light behind her. It revealed her figure as slim and pleasantly graven. The lamp's rays turned her hair into an iridescent halo about her head. She rested one hand against the frame of the door; and her lifted arm guided her body into graceful lines.

She called to them in a low voice, "Do you need light?"

Evered answered. "If you were out of the door there'd be light enough," he said.

The woman lifted her hand to her lips in a hurt little gesture; and she stepped aside with no further word. She still stood thus, at one side of the door, when they came in. The lamplight fell full upon her, full upon her countenance.

The woman's face, the face of this woman whose body still bore youthful lines, was shocking. There were weary contours in it; there were shadows of pain beneath the eyes; there was anguish in the mobile lips. The hair which had seemed like a halo showed now like a white garland; snow white, though it still lay heavy and glossy as a girl's. She was like a statue of sorrow; the figure of a sad and tortured life.

The woman was Evered's second wife; Evered's wife, Mary Evered. His wife, whom he had won in a courtship that was like red flowers in spring; whom he had made to suffer interminably, day by day, till suffering became routine and death would have been happiness; and whom—believe it or no—Evered had always and would forever love with a love that was like torment. There is set perversely in man and woman alike an impulse to tease and hurt and distress those whom we love. It is, of this stuff that lovers' quarrels are made; it is from this that the heartbreaks of the honeymoon are born. The men and women of the fairy tales, who marry and live happily ever after, are fairy tales themselves; or else they never loved. For loving, which is sacrifice and service and kindness and devotion, is also misunderstanding and distortion and perversity and unhappiness most profound. It is a part of love to quarrel; the making-up is often so sweet it justifies the anguish of the conflict. Mary Evered knew this. But Evered had a stiff pride in him which would not let him yield; be he ever so deeply wrong he held his ground; and Mary was sick with much yielding.

Annie Paisley, who lived at the next farm on the North Fraternity road, had given Mary Evered something to think about when Paisley died, the year before.

For over Paisley's very coffin Annie had said in a thoughtful, reminiscent way: "Yes, Mary; Jim 'uz a good husband to me for nigh on thirty year. A good pervider, and a kind man, and a good father. He never drunk, nor ever wasted what little money we got; and we always had plenty to do with; and the children liked him. Kind to me, he was. Gentle." Her eyes had narrowed thoughtfully. "But Mary," she said, "you know I never liked him."

Mary Evered had been a girl of spirit and strength; and if she had not loved Evered she would never have stayed with him a year. Loving him she had stayed; and the bitter years rolled over her; stayed because she loved him, and because she—like her son—understood the heart of the man, and knew that through all his ruthless strength and hard purpose, with all his might he loved her.

She said now in the kitchen: "You got the salt pork?"

"Of course I got the salt pork," Evered told her in a level tone that was like a whip across her shoulders. He dumped his parcels on the table, pointed to one; and she took it up in a hurried furtive way and turned to the stove. John laid down his bundles, and Evered said to him: "Put the horse away." The young man nodded, and went out into the farmyard.

The horse still stood where Evered had bade it stand. John went to the creature's head and laid his hand lightly on the velvety nose, and spoke softly; and after a moment the horse mouthed his hand with its lips. He took the bridle and led it toward the stable. There was a lantern hanging by the door, but he did not light it. The young man loved the still darkness of the night; there was some quality in the damp cool air which was like wine to him. And he needed no light for what he had to do; he knew every wooden peg in the barn's stout frame, blindfolded; for the barn and the farm had been his world for more than twenty years.

Outside the stable door he stopped the horse and loosed the traces and led it out of the thills, which he lowered carefully to the ground. The horse turned, as of habit, to a tub full of water which stood beside the barn door; and while the creature drank John backed the buggy into the carriage shed and propped up the thills with a plank. When he came to the stable door again the horse was waiting for him; and he heard its breath whir in a soundless whinny of greeting. He stripped away the harness expertly, hanging it on pegs against the wall, and adjusted the halter. Once, while he worked, the red bull in its closed stall on the farther side of the barn bellowed softly; and the young man called to the beast in a tone that was at once strong and kindly.

He put the horse in its stall, tied the halter rope, and stepped out into the open floor of the barn to pull down hay for the beast. It was when he did so that he became conscious that someone was near. He could not have told how he knew; but there was, of a sudden, a warmth and a friendliness in the very air about him, so that his breath came a little more quickly. He stood very still for a moment; and then he looked toward the stable door. His eyes, accustomed to the dark, discovered her. She had come inside the barn and was standing against the wall, watching him. He could see the dim white blur of her face in the darkness; he could almost see the glow that lay always in her eyes for him.

He said quietly, "Hello, Ruth."

And she answered him, "Hello, John."

"I've got to pull down a little hay," he said. It was as though he apologized for not coming at once to her side.

"Yes," she told him, and stood there while he finished tending the horse.

When he had done he went toward her slowly and stood before her, and she moved a little nearer to him, so that he put his arms awkwardly round her shoulders and kissed her. He felt her lips move against his; felt her womanly and strong. There was no passion in their caress; only an awkward tenderness on his part, a deep affection on hers.

"I'm glad you came out," he said; and she nodded against his shoulder.

They went into the barnyard, and his arm was about her waist.

"It's warm to-night," she told him. "Summer's about here."

He nodded. "We'll have green peas by the Fourth if we don't git a frost."

Neither of them wanted to get at once to the house. There was youth in them; the house was no place for youth. She was Ruth MacLure, Mary Evered's sister. Not, by that token, John Evered's aunt; for John Evered's mother was dead many years gone, before Evered took Mary MacLure for wife. A year ago old Bill MacLure had died and Ruth had come to live with her sister. John had never known her till then; since then he found it impossible to understand how he had ever lived without knowing her. She was years younger than her sister, three years younger than John Evered himself; and he loved her.

They crossed the barnyard to the fence and looked down into the shadowy pit of blackness where the swamp lay, half a mile below them. They rested their elbows on the top bar of the fence. Once or twice the bull muttered in his stall a few rods away. They could hear the champ of the horse's teeth as the beast fed before sleeping; they could hear Evered's cows stirring in their tie-up. The night was very still and warm, as though heaven brooded like a mother over the earth.

The girl said at last, "Semler was here while you were gone."

The young man asked slowly, "What fetched him here?"

"He was on his way home from fishing, down in the swamp stream."

"Did he do anything down there?"

"Had seventeen. One of them was thirteen inches long. He wanted to leave some, but Mary wouldn't let him."

They were silent for a moment, then John Evered said, "Best not tell my father."

The girl cried under her breath, with an impatient gesture of her hand, "I'm not going to. But I hate it. It isn't fair. Mary wants him to keep away. He bothers her."

"I can keep him away."

"You did tell him not to come."

"I can make him not come," said John Evered; and the girl fell silent, and said at last, "He's writing to her. Oh, John, what can she do? More than she has done?"

"I'll see to't he stays away," the young man promised; and the girl's hand fell on his arm.

"Please do," she said. "He's so unfair to Mary."

A little later, when they turned at last toward the house, John said half to himself, "If my father ever heard, he'd bust that man."

"I wish he would," the girl said hotly. "But—I'm afraid he'd find some way to blame Mary. He mustn't know."

"I'll see Dane Semler," John promised.

On the doorstep they kissed again. Then they went into the house together. Evered sitting by the lamp with his paper looked up at them bleakly, but said no word. Mary Evered smiled at her sister, smiled at John. She loved her husband's son, had loved him like a mother since she came to the house and found him, a boy not four years old, helping with the chores as a grown man might have done. She had found something pitiful in the strength and the reserve of the little fellow; and she had mothered out of him some moments of softness and affection that would have surprised his father.

There was a certain measure of reassurance in his eyes as he returned her smile. But when he had sat down across the table from his father, where she could not see his face, he became sober and very thoughtful. He was considering the matter of Dane Semler.

# CHAPTER IV

FIRST word of the tragedy came to Will Bissell's store at seven o'clock in the evening of the next day but one; and the manner of the coming was this:

The day had been lowering and sultry; such a day as Fraternity was accustomed to expect in mid-August, when the sun was heavy on the land and the air was murky with sea fogs blown in from the bay. A day when there seemed to be a malignant spirit in the very earth itself; a day when to work was torment, and merely to move about was sore discomfort. A day when dogs snarled at their masters, and masters cursed at their dogs; when sullen passions boiled easily to the surface, and tempers were frayed to the last splitting strand.

No breath of air was stirring as the evening came down. The sun had scarce shown itself all day; the coming of night was indicated only by a growing obscurity, by a thickening of the murky shadows in the valleys and the gray clouds that hid the hills. Men slighted their evening chores, did them hurriedly or not at all, and made haste to get into the open air. From the houses of the village they moved toward Will's store; and some of them stopped on the bridge above the brook, as though the sound of running water below them had some cooling power; and some climbed the little slope and sat on the high steps of the store. They talked little or none, spoke in monosyllables when they spoke at all. They were too hot and weary and uncomfortable for talking.

No one seemed to be in any hurry. The men moved slowly; the occasional wagon or buggy that drove into town came at a walk; even the automobiles seemed to move with a sullen reluctance. So it was not surprising that the sound of a horse's running feet coming along the Liberty road should quickly attract their ears.

They heard it first when the horse topped the rise above the mill, almost a mile away. The horse was galloping. The sounds were hushed while the creature dipped into a hollow, and rang more loudly when it climbed a nearer knoll and came on across the level meadow road toward the town. The beat of its hoofs was plainly audible; and men asked each other whose horse it was, and what the hurry might be; and one or two, more energetic than the rest, stood up to get a glimpse of the road by which the beast was coming.

Just before it came into their sight they heard it stop galloping and come on at a trot; and a moment later horse and rider came in sight, and every man saw who it was.

Jean Bubier exclaimed, "It is M'sieu' Semler."

And Judd echoed, "Dane Semler. In a hell of a hurry, too."

Then the man pulled his horse to a stand at the foot of the store steps and swung off. He had been riding bareback; and he was in the garments which he was accustomed to wear when he went fishing along the brooks. They all knew him; for though he was a man of the cities he had been accustomed to come to Fraternity in June for a good many years. They knew him, but did not particularly like him. There was always something of patronage in his attitude, and they knew this and resented it.

Nevertheless, one or two of them answered his greeting. For the rest, they studied him with an acute and painful curiosity. There was some warrant for their curiosity. Semler, usually an immaculate man, was hot and dusty and disordered; his face was white; his eyes were red and shifting, and there was an agonized haste in his bearing which he was unable to hide.

He asked, almost as his foot touched ground, "Anyone here got a car?"

Two or three of the men had come in automobiles; and one, George Tower, answered, "Sure."

Tower was a middle-aged man of the sort that remains perpetually young; and he had recently acquired a swift and powerful roadster of which he was mightily proud. It was pride in this car, more than a desire to help Dane Semler, that prompted his answer.

Semler took a step toward him and lowered his voice a little. "I've had bad news," he said. "How long will it take you to get me to town?"

That was a drive of ten or a dozen miles, over roads none too good.

Tower answered promptly: "Land you there in twenty minutes."

"I'll give you a dollar for every minute you do it under half an hour," said Semler swiftly; and Tower got to his feet.

"Where's your grip?" he asked.

Semler shook his head. "I'm having that sent on. Can't wait. I'm ready to start now." He looked toward the men on the steps. "Some of you take care of the horse," he said quickly. "Garvey will send for it."

Garvey was the farmer at whose house Semler had been staying. Will Bissell took the horse's bridle and promised to stable the beast till Garvey should come. Tower was already in his car; Semler jumped in beside him. They were down the hill and across the bridge in a diminuendo roar of noise as the roadster, muffler cut out, rocketed away toward town. Two or three of the men got to their feet to watch them go, sat down again when they were out of sight.

There was a moment's thoughtful silence before someone said, "What do you make o' that? Semler in some hurry, I'd say."

Jean Bubier laughed a little. "One dam' hurry," he agreed.

"Like something was after him—or he was after someone."

Judd the mean cackled to himself. "By Gad," he cried, "I'll bet Evered's got on to him. I'll bet Evered's after that man. No wonder he run."

The other men looked at Judd, and they shifted uncomfortably. Will Bissell had gone round to stable the horse; Lee Motley had not yet come to the store, nor had Jim Saladine. Lacking these three there was no one to silence Judd, and the man might have gone on to uglier speech.

But he was silenced, and silenced by so inconsiderable a person as Zeke Pitkin. Zeke drove up just then, drove hurriedly; and they saw before he stopped his horse that he was shaking with excitement.

He cried out, "Hain't you heard?"

Judd answered, "Heard what? What ails you, Zeke?"

Pitkin scarce heard him, he was so intent on crying out his dreadful news. It came in a stumbling burst of half a dozen words.

"Evered's red bull's killed Mis' Evered," he stammered.

# CHAPTER V

EVERED'S red bull was a notorious and dangerous figure in the countryside. It was like some primordial monster of the forests, and full as fierce of temper. Evered had bought it two years before, and two men on horseback, with ropes about the creature's neck, brought it from town to his farm. Evered himself, there to receive it, scowled at their precautions. There was a ring in the monstrous beast's nose; and to this ring Evered snapped a six-foot stick of ash, seasoned and strong. Holding the end of this stick he was able to control the bull; and he set himself to teach it fear. That he succeeded was well enough attested. The bull did fear him, and with reason. Nevertheless, Evered took no chances with the brute, and never entered its stall without first snapping his ash stick fast to the nose ring. Those who watched at such times said that the bull's red eyes burned red and redder so long as Evered was near; and those who saw were apt to warn the man to take care. But Evered paid no heed to their warnings; or seemed to pay no heed.

The bull had never harmed a human being, because it had never found the opportunity. Men and women and children shunned it, kept well away from its stout-fenced pasture, its high-boarded pen and its stall. The creature was forever roaring and bellowing; and when the air was still its clamor carried far across the countryside and frightened children and women, and made even men pause to listen and to wonder whether Evered's bull was loose at last. Some boys used to come and take a fearsome joy from watching the brute; and at first they liked to tease the bull, pelting it with sticks and stones. Till one day they came—Jimmy Hills, and Will Motley, and Joe Suter, and two or three besides—with a setter pup of Lee Motley's at their heels. The pup watched their game, and wished to take a hand, so slipped through the fence to nip at the great bull's heels; and the beast wheeled and pinned the dog against the fence with its head like a ram, and then trod the pup into a red pudding in the soft earth, while Will Motley shrieked with rage and sorrow and fear.

Evered heard them that day, and came down with a whip and drove them away; and thereafter a boy who teased the bull had trouble on his hands at home. And the tale of what the brute had done to that setter pup was told and retold in every farmhouse in the town.

Evered, even while he mastered the bull and held it slave, took pains to maintain his dominance. The stall which housed it was stout enough to hold an elephant; the board-walled pen outside the stall was doubly braced with cedar posts set five feet underground; and even the half-mile pasture in which, now and then, he allowed the brute to range, had a double fence of barbed-wire inside and stone wall without.

This pasture ran along the road and bent at right angles to work down to the edge of the swamp. It was, as has been said, about a half mile long; but it was narrow, never more than a few rods wide. It formed the southern boundary of Evered's farm; and no warning signs were needed to keep trespassers from crossing this area. When the bull was loose here it sometimes ranged along the fence that paralleled the road, tossing its great head and snorting and muttering at people who passed by, so that they were apt to hurry their pace and leave the brute behind.

It was timid Zeke Pitkin, on his way to North Fraternity, who saw the bull break its fence on the afternoon that Mary Evered was killed. Zeke did not usually take the road past Evered's place, because he did not like to pass under the eye of the bull. But on this day he was in some haste; and he thought it likely the bull would be stalled and out of sight, and on that chance took the short hill road to his destination.

When he approached Evered's farm he began to hear the bull muttering and roaring in some growing exasperation. But it was then too late to turn back without going far out of his way, so he pressed on until he came in sight of the pasture and saw the beast, head high, tramping up and down along the fence on the side away from the road. Zeke was glad the bull was on that side, and hurried his horse, in a furtive way, hoping the bull would not mark his passing.

When he came up to where the brute was he saw that the bull was watching something in Evered's woodlot, beyond the pasture; and Zeke tried to see what it was. At first he could not see; but after a moment a dog yapped there, and Zeke caught a glimpse of it; a half-bred terrier from some adjacent farm, roving the woods.

The dog yapped; and the bull roared; and the dog, its native impudence impelling it, came running toward the pasture, and began to dance up and down, just beyond the bull's reach, barking in a particularly shrill and tantalizing way.

Zeke yelled to the dog to be off; but the dog took his yell for encouragement, and barked the harder; and then Zeke saw a thing which made him turn cold.

He saw the bull swing suddenly, with all its weight, against the high wire fence; and he saw one of the posts sag and give way, and another smashed off short. So, quicker than it takes to tell it, the bull was floundering across the barbed wires, roaring with the pain of them, and Zeke saw it top the wall, tail high and head down, and charge the little dog.

Zeke might have tried to drive the bull back into its pasture; but that was a task for a bold man, and Zeke was not bold. He whipped his horse and drove on to warn Evered; and when he looked back from the top of the hill the bull and the dog had disappeared into the scrub growth of alder and hardwood along a little run that led down to the swamp. He whipped his horse again, and turned into the road that led to Evered's farmhouse.

When he got to the farmhouse there was no one at home; and after he had convinced himself of this Zeke drove away again, planning to stop at the first neighboring farm and leave word for Evered. But after a quarter of a mile or so he met the butcher, and stopped him and told him that the bull was loose in his woodlot.

Evered asked a question or two; but Zeke's voluble answers made him impatient, and he left the other and hurried on. At home he stabled his horse, got his ash stave with the snap on the end, and as an afterthought went into the house for his revolver. He had no illusions about the bull; he knew the beast was dangerous.

While he was in the house he marked that his wife was not there, and wondered where she was, and called to her, but got no answer. He knew that John and Ruth MacLure, his wife's sister, were in the orchard on the other side of the farm from the pasture and woodlot; and he decided that his wife must have gone to join them there. So with the revolver in his pocket and the stave in his hand, Evered went down past the barn and through the bars into the woodlot. Somewhere in the thickets below him he expected to find the bull. He could hear nothing, so he understood that the little dog which had caused the trouble had either fled or been killed by the beast. He hoped for the latter; for he was an impatient man, and angered at the whole incident. Also, the sultry heat of the day had irked him; irked him so that he had cursed to himself because his wife was not at home when he wished to speak to her.

In this impatient mood he began to work down through the woodlot. He went carefully, knowing the treacherous temper of the brute he was hunting. He passed through a growth of birches along a little run, and across a rocky knoll, and through more birches, and so came out upon the lower shelf of his farm, a quarter of a mile from the house, and halfway down to the borders of the swamp.

He remembered, when he had come thus far, that there was a spring in the hillside a little below him, with two or three old trees above it, and some clean grass beside it. His wife occasionally came here in the afternoon, when her work was done, to sit and read or rest or give herself to her thoughts. Evered knew of this habit of hers; but till this moment he had forgotten it. The spot was cool; it caught what air was stirring. He had a sudden conviction that she might be there now; and the idea angered him. He was angry with her because by coming down here she had put herself in a dangerous position. He was angry with her because he was worried about her safety. This was a familiar reaction of the man's irascible temperament. Two years before, when Mary Evered took to her bed for some three weeks' time with what was near being pneumonia, Evered had been irritable and morose and sullen until she was on her feet again. Unwilling to confess his concern for her, he expressed that concern by harsh words and scowls and bitter taunts, till his wife wept in silent misery. His wife whom he loved wept in misery because of him.

Thus it was now with him. He was afraid she had come to the spring; he was afraid the bull would come upon her there; and because he was afraid for her he was angry with her for coming.

He went forward across the level rocky ground, eyes and ears alert; and so came presently atop a little rise from which he could look down to the spring. And at what he saw the man stopped stock-still, and all the fires of hell flared up in his heart till he felt his whole body burn like a flaming ember.

His wife was there; she was sitting on a low smooth rock a little at one side of the spring. But that was not all; she was not alone. A man sat below her, a little at one side, looking up at her and talking earnestly; and Mary Evered's head was drooping in thought as she listened.

Evered knew the man. The man was Dane Semler. Dane Semler and his wife, together here, talking so quietly.

They did not see him. Their backs were toward him, and they were oblivious and absorbed. Evered stood still for a moment, then he was so shaken by the fury of his own anger that he could not stand, and he dropped on one knee and knelt there, watching them. And the blood boiled in him, and the pulse pounded in his throat, and the breath choked in his lungs. His veins swelled, his face became purple. One watching him would have been appalled.

Evered was in that moment a terrible and dreadful spectacle, a man completely given over to the ugliest of angers, to the black and tempestuous fury of jealousy.

He did not stop to wonder, to guess the meaning of the scene before him. He did not wish to know its explanation. If he had thought soberly he must have known there was no wrong in Mary Evered. But he did not think soberly; he did not think at all. He gave himself to fury. Accustomed to yield to anger as a man yields to alcohol, accustomed to debauches of rage, Evered in this moment loosed all bounds on himself. He hated his wife as it is possible to hate only those whom we love; he hated Dane Semler consumingly, appallingly. He was drunk with it, shaking with it; his lips were so hot it was as though they smoked with rage.

The man and the woman below him did not move. He could catch, through the pounding in his own ears, the murmur of their voices. Semler spoke quickly, rapidly, lifting a hand now and then in an appealing gesture; the woman, when she spoke at all, raised her head a little to look at the man, and her voice was very low. Evered did not hear their words; he did not wish to. The very confidence and ease and intimacy of their bearing damned them unutterably in his eyes.

He was like a figure of stone, there on the knoll just above them. It seemed impossible that they could remain unconscious of his presence there. The unleashed demons in the man seemed to cry out, they were almost audible.

But the two were absorbed; they saw nothing and heard nothing; nothing save each other. And Evered above them, a concentrated fury, was as absorbed and oblivious as they. His whole being was so focused in attention on these two that he did not see the great red bull until it came ponderously round a shoulder of the hill, not thirty paces from where the man and woman sat together. He did not see it then until they turned their heads that way, until they came swiftly to their feet, the man with a cry, the woman in a proud and courageous silence.

The bull stood still, watching them. And in the black soul of Evered an awful triumph leaped and screamed. His ash stave was beside him, his revolver was beneath his hand. There was time and to spare.

He flung one fist high and brought it smashing down. It struck a rock before him and crushed skin and knuckles till the blood burst forth. But Evered did not even know. There was a dreadful exultation in him.

He saw the bull's head drop, saw the vast red bulk lunge forward, quick as light; saw Semler dodge like a rabbit, and run, shrieking, screaming like a woman; saw Mary Evered stand proudly still as still.

In the last moment Evered flung himself on the ground; he hid his face in his arms. And the world rocked and reeled round him so that his very soul was shaken.

Face in his arms there, the man began presently to weep like a little child.

# CHAPTER VI

AFTER an interval, which seemed like a very long time, but was really only a matter of seconds, Evered got to his feet, and with eyes half averted started down the knoll toward the spring.

Yet even with averted eyes he was able to see what lay before him; and a certain awed wonder fell upon the man, so that he was shaken, and stopped for a moment still. And there were tremorous movements about his mouth when he went on.

His wife's body lay where it had been flung by the first blunt blow of the red bull's awful head. But—this was the wonder of it—the red bull had not trampled her. The beast stood above the woman's body now, still and steady; and Evered was able to see that there was no more murder in him. He had charged the woman blindly; but it was now as though, having struck her, he knew who she was and was sorrowing. It was easy to imagine an almost human dejection in the posture of the huge beast.

And it was this which startled and awed Evered; for the bull had always been, to his eyes, an evil and a murderous force.

A few feet from where the woman's body lay Evered stopped and looked at the bull; and the bull stood quite still, watching Evered without hostility. Evered found it hard to understand.

He turned to one side and knelt beside his wife's body; but this was only for an instant. He saw at once that she was dead, beyond chance or question. There was no blood upon her, no agony of torn flesh; her garments were a little rumpled, and that was all. The mighty blow of the bull had been swift enough, and merciful. She lay a little on her side, and her lips were twisted in a little smile, not unhappily.

Evered at this time was not conscious of feeling anything at all. His mind was clear enough; his perceptions were never more acute. But his emotions seemed to be in abeyance. He looked upon his wife's body and felt for her neither the awful hate of the last minutes nor the torturing love of the years that were gone. He looked simply to see if she were dead; and she was dead. So he took off his coat and made of it a pillow for her, and laid her head upon it, and composed her where she lay. And the great red bull stood by, with that unbelievable hint of sorrow and regret in its bearing; stood still as stone, and watched so quietly.

Evered did not think of Semler; he had scarce thought of the man at all, from the beginning. When he was done with his wife he went to where the bull stood, and snapped his ash stave fast to the creature's nose. The bull made no move, neither backed away nor snorted nor jerked aside its vast head. And Evered, his face like a stone, led the beast to one side and up the slope and through the woodlot toward the farm.

As he approached the barn he turned to one side and came to the boarded pen outside the bull's stall. He led the beast inside this pen, loosed the stave from the nose ring, and stepped back outside the gate. Watching for a moment he saw the red bull walk slowly across the pen and go into its stall; and once inside it turned round and stood with its head in the doorway of the stall, watching him.

He made fast the gate, then passed through the barn and approached the kitchen door. Ruth, his wife's sister, came to the door to meet him. His face was steady as a rock; there was no emotion in the man. Yet there was something about him which appalled the girl.

She asked huskily, "Did you get the bull in? I heard him, didn't I?"

"Yes," said Evered. "He's in."

"I heard him bellowing," she explained. "And then I saw a man run up across the side field to the road."

"That was Semler," Evered explained coldly. "Dane Semler. He was afraid of the bull."

"I was worried," the girl persisted timidly, not daring to say what was in her mind. "I was worried—worried about Mary."

"The bull killed her," said Evered; and passed her and went into the kitchen.

Ruth backed against the wall to let him go by; and she pressed her two hands to her lips in a desperate frightened way; and her eyes were wide and staring with horror. She stared at the man, and her hands held back the clamor of her grief. She stared at him as at a monstrous thing, while Evered washed his hands at the sink and dried them on the roller towel, and combed his hair before the clean mirror hanging on the wall. There was a dreadful deliberation about his movements.

After a moment the girl began to move; she went by little sidewise steps as far as the door, and then she leaped out into the barnyard, and the screams poured from her in a frenzy of grief that was half madness. Evered turned at the first sound and watched her run, still screaming, across the barnyard to the fence; and he saw her fumble fruitlessly with the topmost bars, and at last scramble awkwardly over the fence itself in her stricken haste. She was still crying out terribly as she disappeared from his sight in the direction of the woodlot and the spring.

Evered watching her said to himself bitterly: "She knew where Mary was; knew where to look for her."

He flung out one hand in a weak gesture of despair that came strangely from so harshly strong a man; and he began to move aimlessly about the kitchen, not knowing what he did. He took a drink at the pump; he changed his shoes for barnyard boots; he cut tobacco from a plug and filled his pipe and forgot to light it; he stood in the door, the cold pipe in his teeth, and stared out across his farm; and his teeth set on the pipestem till it cracked and roused him from his own thoughts.

Then he heard someone running, and his son, John Evered, came from the direction of the orchard, and flung a quick glance at his father, and another into the kitchen at his father's back.

Evered looked at him, and the young man, panting from his run, said, "I heard Ruth cry out. What's happened, father?"

Evered's tight lips did not stir for a moment; then he took the pipe in his hand, and he said stiffly, "The red bull killed Mary."

They were accustomed to speak of Evered's second wife as Mary when they spoke together. John, though he loved her, had never called her mother. He loved her well; but the blood tie was strong in him, and he loved his father more. At his father's word now he stepped nearer the older man, watching, sensing something of the agony behind Evered's simple statement; and their eyes met and held for a little.

Then Evered said, "She was with Dane Semler at the spring."

The gentler lines of his son's face slowly hardened into a likeness of his own. The young man asked, "Where's Semler?"

"Ran away," said Evered.

"I had wanted a word with him."

Evered laughed shortly; and it was almost the first time that John had ever seen him laugh, so that the sight was shocking and terrible. Then the older man turned back into the house.

John followed him and asked quickly, "It was at the spring?"

"Yes. The bull broke down his fence to get at a dog."

"We must bring her home," the son suggested quietly. "Where is Ruth?"

"Down there," Evered told him.

John turned to the door again. "We'll bring her home," he said; and Evered saw the young man go swiftly across the farmyard and vault the fence and start at an easy run in the direction Ruth had gone.

Evered stayed in the house alone for a moment; and when he could bear to be alone no longer he went out into the farmyard. As he did so Zeke Pitkin drove in, on his way back from that errand in North Fraternity.

The bleak face of Evered appalled the timid man and frightened him; and he stammered apologetically: "W-wondered if you got the b-bull in."

"Yes," said Evered. "After he had killed Mary."

Zeke stared at Evered with a face that was a mask of terror for a moment, and Evered stood still, watching him. Then Pitkin gathered his reins clumsily, and clumsily turned his horse, so sharply that his wagon was well-nigh overthrown by the cramped wheel. When it was headed for the road he lashed out with the whip, and the horse leaped forward. Evered could hear it galloping out to the main road, and then to the left, toward Fraternity.

"Town'll know in half an hour," he said half to himself.

The man was still in a stupor, his emotions numb. But he did not want to be alone. After a moment he went out into the stable and harnessed the horse to his light wagon and started down a wood road toward the spring. The wagon would serve to bring his wife's body home.

The vehicles on a Fraternity farm are there for utility, almost without exception. Evered had a mowing machine, a rake, a harrow, a sledge, a single-seated buggy and this light wagon. He was accustomed to take the wagon when he went butchering; and it had served to haul the carcasses of any number of sheep or calves or pigs or steers from farm to market. He had no thought that he was piling horror on horror in taking this wagon to bring home his wife's body.

He laid a double armful of hay in the bed of the wagon before he started; and he himself walked by the horse's head, easing it over the rough places. The wood road which he followed would take him within two or three rods of the spring.

John Evered, going before his father, had found Ruth MacLure passionately sobbing above the body of her sister. And at first he could not bring himself to draw near to her; he was held by some feeling that to approach her would be sacrilege. There had been such a love between the sisters as is not often seen; there was a spiritual intimacy between them, a sympathy of mind and heart akin to that sometimes marked between twins. John knew this; he knew all that Ruth's grief must be. And so he stood still, a little ways off from her, and waited till the tempest of her grief should pass.

When she was quieter he spoke to her; and at the sound of his voice the girl whirled to face him, still kneeling; and there were no more tears in her. He was frightened at the stare of challenge in her eyes. He said quickly, "It's me."

She shook her head as though something blurred her sight. "I thought it was your father," she told him, and there was a bitter condemnation in her tone.

John said, "You mustn't blame him."

"He's not even sorry," she explained softly, thoughtfully.

"He is," John insisted. "You never understood him. He loved her so."

She flung her head to one side impatiently and got to her feet, brushing at her eyes with her sleeve, fumbling with her hair, composing her countenance. "It's growing dark," she said. "We must take her home."

He nodded. "I'll carry her," he said; and he crossed and bent above the dead woman, and looked at her for a moment silently. The girl, watching him, saw in the still strength of his features a likeness to his father that was suddenly terrible and appalling.

She shuddered; and when he would have lifted her sister's body she cried out in passionate hysterical protest, "Don't touch her! Don't touch her! You shan't touch her, John Evered!"

John looked at her slowly; and with that rare understanding which was the birthright of the man he said, "You're blaming father."

"Yes, yes," she cried, "I am."

"It was never his fault," he said.

"He kept that red, killing brute about," she protested. "Oh, he killed her, he killed Mary, he killed my sister, John."

"That is not fair," he told her.

Before she could answer they both hushed to the sound of the approaching wagon; and Evered came toward them, leading the horse, and he turned it and backed the wagon in below the spring.

They did not speak to him, nor he to them. But when he was ready he went toward the dead woman to lift her into the wagon bed; and Ruth pushed between them and cried: "You shan't touch her! You shan't touch her, ever!"

Evered looked at her steadily; and after a moment he said, "Stand to one side."

The girl wished to oppose him; but it was a tribute to his strength that even in this moment the sheer will of the man overpowered her. She moved aside; and Evered lifted his wife's body with infinite gentleness and disposed it upon the fragrant hay in the wagon bed. He put the folded coat again beneath his wife's head as a pillow, as though she were only sleeping.

Still with no word to them he took the horse's rein and started to lead it toward the road and up the hill. And Ruth and John, after a moment, followed a little behind.

When they came up into the open, out of the scattering trees, a homing crow flying overhead toward its roost saw them. It may have been that the wagon roused some memory in the bird, offered it some promise. At any rate, the black thing circled on silent wing, and lighted in the road along which they had come, and hopped and flopped behind them as they went slowly up the hill toward the farm.

Ruth saw the bird and shuddered; and John went back and drove it into flight; but it took earth again, farther behind them.

It followed them insistently up the hill; and it was still there, a dozen rods away, as they brought Mary Evered home.

# CHAPTER VII

WHEN they came into the farmyard night was falling. In the west the sky still showed bright and warm; and against this brilliant sky the hills were purple and deeper purple in the distance. In the valleys mists were rising and black pools of night were forming beneath these mists; and while Evered bore his wife's body into the house and laid it on the bed in the spare room, these pools rose and rose until they topped the hills and overflowed the world with darkness. The air was still hot and heavy, as it had been all day; and the sultry sky which had intensified the heat of the sun served now to hide the stars. When it grew dark it was as dark as pitch. The blackness seemed tangible, as though a man might catch it in his hand.

Ruth stayed beside her sister; but John built a fire in the stove while Evered sat by in stony calm, and he made coffee and fried salt pork and boiled potatoes. There were cold biscuits which Mary Evered had made that morning, and doughnuts from the crock in the cellar. When the supper was ready he called Ruth; and she came. The most tragic thing about death is that it accomplishes so little. The dropping of man or woman into the pool of the infinite is no more than the dropping of a pebble into a brook. The surface of the pool is as calm, a little after, as it was before. Thus, now, save that Mary was not at the table, their supping together was as it had always been.

And after they had eaten they must go with the familiarity of long habit about their evening chores. Ruth washed the dishes; John and his father fed the beasts and milked the cows; and when they came in John turned the separator while Ruth attended to the milk and put away, afterward, the skim milk and the cream.

By that time two or three neighbors had come in, having heard of that which had come to pass. There was genuine sorrow in them, for Mary Evered had been a woman to be loved; but there was also the ugly curiosity native to the human mind; and there was speculation in each eye as they watched Evered and John and Ruth. They would discuss, for days to come, the bearing of each one of the three on that black night.

For Evered, the man was starkly silent, saying no word. He sat by the table, eyes before him, puffing his pipe. Ruth stayed by her sister as though some instinct of protection kept her there. John talked with those who came, told them a little. He did not mention Semler's part in the tragedy. He said simply that the bull had broken loose; that Mary Evered was by the spring, where she liked to go; that the bull came upon her there.

They asked morbidly whether she was trampled and torn; and they seemed disappointed when he told them that she was not, that even the terrible red bull had seemed appalled at the thing which he had done. And through the evening others came and went, so that he had to say the same things over and over; and always Evered sat silently by the table, giving no heed when any man spoke to him; and Ruth, in the other room, kept guard above the body. The women went in there, some of them; but no men went in.

John had telephoned to Isaac Gorfinkle, whose business it was to prepare poor human clay for its return to earth again; and Gorfinkle came about midnight and put all save Ruth out of the room where the dead woman lay. Gorfinkle was a little, fussy man; a man who knew his doleful trade. Before day he and Ruth had done what needed doing; and Mary Evered lay in the varnished coffin he had brought. Her white hair and the sweet nobility of her countenance, serenely lying there, made those who looked forget the ugly splendor of Gorfinkle's wares.

It was decided that she should be buried on the second day. On the day after her death many people came to the farm; and some came from curiosity, and some from sympathy, and some with an uncertain purpose in their minds.

These were the selectmen of the town—Lee Motley, chairman; and Enoch Thomas, of North Fraternity; and Old Man Varney. Motley, a sober man and a man of wisdom, was of Evered's own generation; Enoch Thomas and Varney were years older. Old Varney had a son past thirty, whom to this day he thrashed with an ax stave when the spirit moved him, his big son good-naturedly accepting the outrage.

Thomas and Varney came to demand that Evered kill his red bull; and Motley put the case for them.

"We've talked it over," he said. "Seem's like the bull's dangerous; like he ought to be killed. That's what we've—what we've voted."

Evered turned his heavy eyes from man to man; and Old Varney brandished his cane and called the bull a murdering beast, and bade Evered take his rifle and do the thing before their eyes. Evered's countenance changed no whit; he looked from Varney to Thomas, who was silent, and from Thomas to Lee Motley.

"I'll not kill the bull," he said.

Before Motley could speak, Varney burst into abuse and insistent demand; and Evered let him talk. When the old man simmered to silence they waited for Evered to answer, but Evered held his tongue till Lee Motley asked, "Come, Evered, what do you say?"

"What I have said," Evered told them.

"The town'll see," Old Varney shrilled, and shook his fist in Evered's face. "The town'll see whether a murdering brute like that is to range abroad. If you've not shame enough—your own wife, man—your own——" he wagged his head. "The town'll see."

Said Evered: "I'll not take rifle to the bull; but if any man comes here to kill the beast, I'll have use for that rifle of mine."

Which fanned Varney to a fresh outbreak, till Evered flung abruptly toward him, and abruptly said, "Be still."

So were they still; and Evered looked them in the eye, man by man, till he came to Motley; and then he said, "Motley, I thought there was more wisdom in you."

"Aye," cried Varney. "He's as big a fool as you."

And Motley said, "I voted against this, Evered. The bull's yours, if you're a mind to kill him. I'm not for making you. It's your own affair, you mind. And—the ways of a bull are the ways of a bull. The brute's not overmuch to be blamed."

Evered nodded and turned his back on them; and after a time they went away. But when Evered went into the house he met Ruth, and the girl stopped him and asked him huskily, "You're not going to kill that red beast?"

Evered hesitated; then he said, with something like apology in his tones, "No, Ruth."

She began to tremble, and he saw that words were hot on her lips; and he lifted one hand in a placating gesture. She turned into the other room, and the door shut harshly at her back. Evered's eyes rested on the door for a space, a curious questioning in them, a wistful light that was strange to see.

All that day Ruth was still, saying little. No word passed between her and Evered, and few words between her and John. But that night, when they were alone, John spoke to her in awkward comfort and endearment.

"Please, Ruthie," he begged. "You're breaking yourself. You'll be sick. You must not be so hard."

He put an arm about her, as though he would have kissed her; but the girl's hands came up against his chest, and the girl's eyes met his in a fury of horror and loathing, and she flung him away.

"Don't! Don't!" she cried in a voice that was like a scream. "Don't ever! You—his son!"

John, inexpressibly hurt, yet understanding, left her alone; he told himself she was not to be blamed, with the agony of grief still scourging her.

One of the neighbor women came in that night to sit with Ruth; and Ruth slept a little through the night. John was early abed; he had had no sleep the night before, and he was tired. He sank fathoms deep in slumber; a slumber broken by fitful, unhappy dreams. His own grief for the woman who had been mother to him had been stifled, given no chance for expression, because he had fought to comfort Ruth and to ease his father. The reaction swept over him while he slept; he rested little.

Evered, about nine o'clock, went to the room he and his wife had shared for so many years. He had not, before this, been in the room since she was killed. Some reluctance had held him; he had shunned the spot. But now he was glad to be alone, and when he had shut the door he stood for a moment, looking all about, studying each familiar object, his nerves reacting to faint flicks of pain at the memories that were evoked.

He began to think of what the selectmen had said, of their urgency that he should kill the bull. And he sat down on the edge of the bed and remained there, not moving, for a long time. Once his eye fell on his belt hanging against the wall, with the heavy knife that he used in his butchering in its sheath. He reached out and took down the belt and drew the knife forth and held it in his hands, the same knife that had killed drunken Dave Riggs long ago. A powerful weapon, it would strike a blow like an ax; the handle of bone, the blade heavy and keen and strong. He balanced it between his fingers, and thought of how he had struck it into the neck of Zeke Pitkin's bull, and how the bull had dropped in midlife and never stirred more. The knife fascinated him; he could not for a long time take his eyes away from it. At the last he reached out and thrust it into its sheath with something like a shudder, strange to see in so strong a man.

Then he undressed and got into bed, the bed he had shared with Mary Evered. He had blown out the lamp; the room was dark. There was a little current of air from the open window. And after a little Evered began to be as lonely as a boy for the first time away from home.

There is in every man, no matter how stern his exterior, a softer side. Sometimes he hides it from all the world; more often his wife gets now and then a glimpse of it. There was a side of Evered which only Mary Evered had known. And she had loved it. When they had come to bed together it always seemed to her that Evered was somehow gentler, kinder. He put away his harshness, as though it were a part he had felt called upon to play before men. The child in him, strong in most men, came to the surface. He was never a man overgiven to caresses, but when they were alone at night together, and he was weary, he would sometimes draw her arm beneath his head as a pillow or take her hand and lift it to rest upon his forehead, while she twined her fingers gently through his hair.

They used to talk together, sometimes far into the night; and though he might have used her bitterly through the day, with caustic tongue and hard, condemning eye, he was never unkind in these moments before they slept. A man the world outside had never seen. It was these nights together which had made life bearable for Mary Evered; and they had been dear to Evered too. How dreadful and appalling, then, was this, his first night alone.

Her shoulder was not there to cradle his sick and weary head; her gentle hand was not there to cool his brow. When he flung an arm across her pillow, where she used to lie, it embraced a gulf of emptiness that seemed immeasurably deep and terrible. After a little, faint perspiration came out upon the man's forehead. He turned on his right side, in the posture that invited sleep; but at first sleep would not come. His limbs jerked and twitched; his eyelids would not close. He stared sightlessly into the dark. Outside in the night there were faint stirrings and scratchings and movings to and fro; and each one brought him more wide awake than the last. He got up and closed the window to shut them out, and it seemed to him the closed room was filled with her presence. When he lay down again he half fancied he felt her hand upon his hair, and he reached his own hand up to clasp and hold hers, as he had sometimes used to do; but his groping fingers found nothing, and came sickly away again.

How long he lay awake he could not know. When at last he dropped asleep the very act of surrender to sleep seemed to fetch him wide awake again. Waking thus he thought that he held his wife in his arms; he had often wakened in the past to find her there. But as his senses cleared he found that the thing which he held so tenderly against his side was only the pillow on which her head was used to lie.

The man's nerves jangled and clashed; and he threw the pillow desperately away from him as though he were afraid of it. He sat up in bed; and his pulses pounded and beat till they hurt him like the blows of a hammer. There was no sleep in Evered.

He was still sitting thus, bolt upright, sick and torn and weary, when the gray dawn crept in at last through the window panes.

# CHAPTER VIII

THE day of Mary Evered's burial was such a day as comes most often immediately after a storm, when the green of the trees is washed to such a tropical brightness that the very leaves radiate color and the air is filled with glancing rays of light. There were white clouds in the blue sky; clouds not dense and thick, but lightly frayed and torn by the winds of the upper reaches, and scudding this way and that according to the current which had grip of them. Now and then these gliding clouds obscured the sun; and the sudden gloom made men look skyward, half expecting a burst of rain. But for the most part the sun shone steadily enough; and there was an indescribable brilliance in the light with which it bathed the earth. Along the borders of the trees, round the gray hulks of the bowlders, and fringing the white blurs of the houses there seemed to shimmer a halo of colors so faint and fine they could be sensed but not seen by the eye. The trees and the fields were an unearthly gaudy green; the shadows deep amid the branches were trembling, changing pools of color. A day fit to bewitch the eye, with a soft cool wind stirring everywhere.

Evered himself was early about, attending to the morning chores. Ruth MacLure had fallen asleep toward morning, and the woman with her let the girl rest. John woke when he heard his father stirring; and it was he who made breakfast ready, when he had done his work about the barn. He and his father ate together, and Ruth did not join them.

Evered, John saw, was more silent than his usual silent custom; and the young man was not surprised, expecting this. John himself, concerned for Ruth, and wishing he might ease the agony of her grief, had few words to say. When they were done eating he cleared away the dishes and washed them and put them away; and then he swept the floor, not because it needed sweeping, but because he could not bear to sit idle, doing nothing at all. He could hear the women stirring in the other room; and once he heard Ruth's voice.

John's grief was more for the living than for the dead; he had loved Mary Evered truly enough, but there was a full measure of philosophy in the young man. She was dead; and according to the simple trust which was a part of him she was happy. But Ruth was unhappy, and his father was unhappy. He wished he might comfort them.

Evered at this time was soberly miserable; his mind was still numb, his emotions were just beginning to assert themselves. He could not think clearly, could scarce think at all. What passed for thought with him was merely a jumble of exclamations, passionate outcries, curses and laments. Mary was dead; and he knew that dimly, without full comprehension of the knowledge. More clearly he remembered Mary and Dane Semler, sitting so intimately side by side; and the memory was compounded of anguish and of satisfaction—anguish because she was false, satisfaction because her frailty in some small measure justified the monstrous thing he had permitted, and in permitting had done. Evered did not seek to deceive himself; he knew that he had killed Mary Evered as truly as he had killed Dave Riggs many a year ago. He did not put the knowledge into words; nevertheless, it was there, in the recesses of his mind, concrete and ever insistent. And when sorrow and remorse began to prick at him with little pins of fire he told himself, over and over, that she had been frail, and so got eased of the worst edge of pain.

A little after breakfast people began to come to the house. Isaac Gorfinkle was first of them all, and he busied himself with his last ugly preparations. Later the minister came—a boy, or little more; fresh from theological school. His name was Mattice, and he was as prim and meticulous as the traditional maiden lady who is so seldom found in life. He tried to speak unctuous comfort to Evered, but the man's scowl withered him; he turned to John, and John had to listen to him with what patience could be mustered. And more men came, and stood in groups about the farmyard, smoking, spitting, shaving tiny curls of wood from splinters of pine; and their women went indoors and herded in the front room together, and whispered and sobbed in a hissing chorus indescribably horrible. There is no creation of mankind so hideous as a funeral; there is nothing that should be more beautiful. The hushed voices, the damp scent of flowers, the stifling closeness of tight-windowed rooms, the shuffling of feet, the raw snuffles of those who wept—these sounds filled the house and came out through the open doors to the men, whispering in little groups outside.

Ruth MacLure was not weeping; nor Evered; nor John. And the mourning, sobbing women kissed Ruth and called her brave; and they whispered to each other that Evered was hard, and that John was like his father. And the lugubrious debauch of tears went on interminably, as though Gorfinkle—whose duty it would be to give the word when the time should come—thought these preliminaries were requisites to a successful funeral.

But at last it was impossible to wait longer without going home for dinner, and Gorfinkle, who was accustomed to act as organist on such occasions, took his seat, pumped the treadles and began to play. Then everyone crowded into the front room or stood in the hall; and a woman sang, and young Mattice spoke for a little while, dragging forth verse after verse of sounding phrase which rang nobly even in his shrill and uncertain tones. More singing, more tears. A blur of pictures photographed themselves on Ruth's eyes; words that she would never forget struck her ears in broken phrases. She sat still, steady and quiet. But her nerves were jangling; and it seemed to the girl she must have screamed aloud if the thing had not ended when it did.

Then the mile-long drive to the hilltop above Fraternity, with its iron fence round about, and the white stones within; and there the brief and solemn words, gentle with grief and glorious with triumphant hope, were spoken above the open grave. And the first clod fell. And by and by the last; and those who had come began to drift away to their homes, to their dinners, to the round of their daily lives.

Evered and John and Ruth drove home together in their light buggy, and Ruth sat on John's knee. But there was no yielding in her, there was no softness about the girl. And no word was spoken by any one of them upon the way.

At home, alighting, she went forthwith into the house; and John put the horse up, while his father fed the pigs and the red bull in his stall. When they were done Ruth called them to dinner, appearing for an instant at the kitchen door. John reached the kitchen before his father; and the pain in him made him speak to the girl before Evered came.

"Ruthie," he said softly. "Please don't be too unhappy."

She looked at him with steady eyes, a little sorrowful. "I'm not unhappy, John," she said. "Because Mary is not unhappy, now. Don't think about me."

"I can't help thinking about you," he told her; and she knew what was behind his words, and shook her head.

"You'll have to help it," she said.

"Why, Ruthie," he protested, "you know how I feel about you."

Her eyes shone somberly. "It's no good, John," she answered. "You're too much Evered. I can see clearer now."

They had not, till then, marked Evered himself in the doorway. Ruth saw him and fell silent; and Evered asked her in a low steady voice, "You're blaming me?"

"I'm cursing you," said the girl.

Evered held still for a little, as though it were hard for him to muster words. Then he asked huskily, "What was my fault?"

She flung up her hand. "Everything!" she cried. "I've lived here with you. I've seen you—breaking Mary by inches, and nagging and teasing and pestering her. Till she was sick with it. And she kept loving you, so you could hurt her more. And you did. You loved to hurt her. Hard and cruel and mean and small—you'd have beat her as you do your beasts, if you'd dared. Coward too. Oh!"

She flung away, began to move dishes aimlessly about upon the table. Evered was gripped by a desire to placate her, to appease her; he thought of Dane Semler, wished to cry out that accusation against his wife. But he held his tongue. He had seen Semler with Mary; he had told John; Ruth knew that Semler had been upon the farm. But neither of them spoke of the man, then or thereafter. They told no one; and though Fraternity might wonder and conjecture, might guess at the meaning of Semler's swift flight on the day of the tragedy, the town would never know.

Evered did not name Semler now; and it was not any sense of shame that held his tongue. He believed wholly in that which his eyes had seen, and all that it implied. Himself scarce knew why he did not speak; and he would never have acknowledged that it was desire to shield his wife, even from her own sister, which kept him silent. After a moment he sat down and they began to eat.

Toward the end of the meal he said to Ruth uneasily: "Feeling so, you'll not be like to stay here with John and me."

Ruth looked at him with a quick flash of eyes; she was silent, thoughtfully. She had not considered this; had not considered what she was to do. But instantly she knew.

"Yes, I'm going to stay," she told Evered. "This thing isn't done. There's more to come. It must be so. For all you did there's something that will come to you. I want to be here, to see." Her hands clenched on the table edge. "I want to see you when it comes—see you squirm and crawl."

There was such certainty in her tone that Evered, spite of himself, was shaken. He answered nothing; and the girl said again, "Yes; I am going to stay."

The red bull in his stall bellowed aloud; a long, rumbling, terrible blare of challenge. It set the dishes dancing on the table before them; and when they listened they could hear the monstrous beast snorting in his stall.

# CHAPTER IX

AFTER the death of Mary Evered the days slipped away, and June passed to July, and July to August. Gardens prospered; the hay ripened in the fields; summer was busy with the land. But winter is never far away in these northern hills; and once in July and twice in August the men of the farms awoke in early morning to find frost faintly lying, so that there were blackened leaves in the gardens, and the beans had once to be replanted. Customary hazards of their arduous life.

The trout left quick water and moved into the deep pools; and a careful fisherman, not scorning the humble worm, might strip a pool if he were murderously inclined. The summer was dry; and as the brooks fell low and lower little fingerlings were left gasping and flopping upon the gravel of the shallows here and there. Nick Westley, the game warden for the district, and a Fraternity man, went about with dip net and pail, bailing penned trout from tiny shallows and carrying them to the larger pools where they might have a chance for life. Some of the more ardent fishermen imitated him; and some took advantage of the trout's extremity to bring home catches they could never have made in normal times.

John Evered loved fishing; and he knew the little brook along the hither border of Whitcher Swamp, below the farm, as well as he knew his own hand. But this year had been busy; he found no opportunity to try the stream until the first week of July. One morning then, with steel rod and tiny hooks, and a can of bait at his belt, he struck down through the woodlot, past the spring where Mary had been killed, into the timber below, and so came to the wall that was the border of his father's farm, and crossed into the swamp.

Whitcher Swamp is on the whole no pleasant place for a stroll; yet it has its charms for the wild things, and for this reason John loved it. Where he struck the marshy ground it was relatively easy going; and he took a way he knew and came to the brook and moved along it a little ways to a certain broad and open pool.

He thought the brook was lower than he had ever seen it at this season; and once he knelt and felt the water, and found it warm. He smiled at this with a certain gratification for the pool he sought was a spring hole, water bubbling up through pin gravel in the brook's very bed, and the trout would be there to dwell in that cooler stream. When he came near the place, screened behind alders so that he could not be seen, he uttered an exclamation, and became as still as the trees about him while he watched.

There were trout in the pool, a very swarm of them, lying close on the yellow gravel bottom. The water, clear as crystal, was no more than three feet deep; and he could see them ever so plainly. Big fat fish, monsters, if one considered the brook in which he found them. He judged them all to be over nine inches, several above a foot, one perhaps fourteen inches long; and his eyes were shining. They were so utterly beautiful, every line of their graceful bodies, and every dappled spot upon their backs and sides as clear as though he held them in his hands.

He rigged line and hook, nicked a long worm upon the point, and without so much as shaking an alder branch thrust his rod through and swung the baited hook and dropped it lightly in the very center of the pool, full fifteen feet from shore. Then he swung upward with a strong steady movement, for he had seen a great trout strike as the worm touched the water, had seen the chewing jaws of the fish mouthing its titbit. And as he swung, the gleaming body came into the air, through an arc above his head, into the brush behind him, where he dropped on his knees beside it and gave it merciful death with the haft of his heavy knife, and dropped it into his basket.

Fly fishermen will laugh with a certain scorn; or they will call John Evered a murderer. Nevertheless, it is none so easy to take trout even in this crude fashion of his. A shadow on the water, a stirring of the bushes, a too-heavy tread along the bank—and they are gone. Nor must they be hurried. The capture of one fish alarms the rest; the capture of two disturbs them; the taking of three too quickly will send them flying every whither.

John, after his first fish, filled and lighted his pipe, then caught a second; and after another interval, a third—fat, heavy trout, all of them; as much as three people would care to eat; and John was not minded to kill more than he could use. He covered the three with wet moss in his basket, and then he crept back through the alders and lay for a long time watching the trout in the pool, absorbing the beauty of their lines, watching how they held themselves motionless with faintest quivers of fin, watching how they fed.

A twelve-inch trout rose and struck at a leaf upon the pool's surface, and John told himself, "They're hungry." He laughed a little, and got an inch-long twig and tied it to the end of his line in place of hook. This he cast out upon the pool, moving it to and fro erratically. Presently a trout swirled up and took it under, and spat it out before John could twitch the fish to the surface. John laughed aloud, and cast again. He stayed there for a long hour at this sport, and when the trout sulked he teased them with bits of leaf or grass. Once he caught a cricket and noosed it lightly and dropped it on the water. When the fish took it down John waited for an instant, then tugged and swung the trout half a dozen feet into the air before he could disgorge the bait.

"Hungry as sin," John told himself at last; and his eyes became sober as he considered thoughtfully. There were other men about, as good fishermen as he, and not half so scrupulous. If they should come upon this pool on such a day——

He did a thing that might seem profanation to the fisherman who likes a goodly bag. He gathered brush and threw it into the pool; he piled it end to end and over and over; he found two small pines; dead in their places among their older brethren; and he pushed them from their rotting roots and dragged them to the brook and threw them in. When he was done the pool was a jungle, a wilderness of stubs and branches; a sure haven for trout, a spot almost impossible to fish successfully. While he watched, when his task was finished, he saw brown darting shadows in the stream as the trout shot back into the covert he had made; and he smiled with a certain satisfaction.

"They'll have to fish for them now," he told himself.

He decided to try and see whether a man might take a trout from the pool in its ambushed state. It meant an hour of waiting, a snagged hook or two, a temper-trying ordeal with mosquitoes and flies. But in the end he landed another fish, and was content. He went back through the swamp and up to the farm, well pleased.

Moving along the brook he saw other pools where smaller fish were lying; and that night he told Ruth what he had seen. "You can see all the trout you're minded to, down there now," he said.

The girl nodded unsmilingly. She had not yet learned to laugh again, since her sister's death. They were a somber household, these three—Evered steadily silent, the girl sober and stern, John striving in his awkward fashion to win mirth from her and speech from Evered.

The early summer was to pass thus. And what was in Evered's mind as the weeks dragged by no man could surely know. His eye was as hard as ever, his voice as harsh; yet to Ruth it seemed that new lines were forming in his cheeks, and his hair, that had been black as coal, she saw one afternoon was streaked with gray. Watching, thereafter, she marked how the white hairs increased in number. Once she spoke of it to John, constrainedly, for there was no such pleasant confidence between these two as there had been.

John nodded. "Yes," he said, "he's aging. He loved her, Ruth; loved her hard."

Ruth made no comment, but there was no yielding in her eyes. She was in these days implacable; and Evered watched her now and then with something almost pleading in his gaze. He began to pay her small attentions, which came absurdly from the man. She tried to hate him for them.

Once John sought to comfort his father, spoke to him gently of the dead woman; and Evered cried out, as though to assure himself as well as silence John: "She was tricking me, John! Leaving me. With Semler, that very day."

He would not let John reply, silenced him with a fierce oath and flung away. It might have been guessed that his belief in his wife's treachery was like an anchor to which Evered's racked soul clung; as though he found comfort and solace in the ugly thought, a justifying consolation.

# CHAPTER X

JOHN went no more to the brooks that summer; but what he had told Ruth led her that way more than once. Westley, the game warden, stopped at the house one day, and found her alone, and asked her whether John was fishing. She told him of John's one catch.

"Swamp Brook is full of trout," she said; "penned in the holes and the shallows."

Westley nodded. "It's so everywhere," he agreed. "I'm dipping and shifting them. Tell John to do that down in the swamp if he can find the time."

She asked how it should be done; and when Westley had gone she decided that she would herself go down and try the trick of it if the drought still held.

The drought held. No rain came; and once in early August she spent an afternoon along the stream, and transported scores of tiny trout to feeding grounds more deep and more secure. Again a week later; and still again as the month drew to a close.

It was on this third occasion that the girl came upon Darrin. Working along the brook with dip net and pail she had marked the footprints of a man in the soft earth here and there. The swamp was still, no air stirring, the humming of insects ringing in her ears. A certain gloom dwelt in these woods even on the brightest day; and the black mold bore countless traces and tracks of the animals and the small vermin which haunted the place at night. Ruth might have been forgiven for feeling a certain disquietude at sight of those man tracks in the wild; but she had no such thought. She had never learned to be afraid.

She came upon Darrin at last with an abruptness that startled her. The soft earth muffled her footsteps; she was within two or three rods of him before she saw him, and even then the man had not heard her. He was kneeling by the brook and at first she thought he had been drinking the water. Then she saw that he was studying something there upon the ground; and a moment later he got up and turned and saw her standing there. At first he was so surprised that he could not speak, and they were still, looking at each other. The girl, bareheaded, in simple waist and heavy short skirt, with rubber boots upon her feet so that she might wade at will, was worth looking at. The man himself was no mean figure—khaki flannel shirt, knickerbockers, leather putties over stout waterproof shoes. She carried pail in one hand, dip net in the other; and she saw that he had a revolver slung in one hip, a camera looped over his shoulder.

He said at last, "Hello, there!" And Ruth nodded in the sober fashion that was become her habit. The man asked, "What have you got? Milk, in that pail? Is this your pasture land?"

"Trout," she told him; and he came to see the fish in a close-packed mass; and he exclaimed at them, and watched while she put them into the stream below where he had been kneeling. He asked her why she did it, and she told him. At the same time she looked toward where he had knelt, wondering what he saw there. She could see only some deep-imprinted moose tracks; and moose tracks were so common in the swamp that it was not worth while to kneel to study them.

He saw her glance, and said, "I was looking at those tracks. Moose, aren't they?"

She nodded. "Yes."

"They told me there were moose in here," he said. "I doubted it, though. So far south as this."

"There are many moose in the swamp," she declared.

He asked, "Have you ever seen them?"

She smiled a little. "Once in a while. A cow moose wintered in our barn two years ago."

He slapped his thigh lightly. "Then this is the place I'm looking for," he exclaimed.

She asked softly, "Why?" She was interested in the man. He was not like John, not like anyone whom she had known; except, perhaps, Dane Semler. A man of the city, obviously. "Why?" she asked.

"I want to get some pictures of them," he explained. "Photographs. In their natural surroundings. Wild. In the swamp."

"John took a snapshot of the cow that wintered with us," she said. "I guess he'd give you one."

The man laughed. "I'd like it," he told her; "but I want to get a great many." He hesitated. "Where is your farm?"

She pointed out of the swamp toward the hill.

"Near?" he asked.

And she said, "It's right over the swamp."

"Listen," he said eagerly. "My name's Darrin—Fred Darrin. What's yours?"

"Ruth MacLure."

"Why you're Evered's sister-in-law, aren't you?"

She nodded, her cheeks paling a little. "Yes."

"I was coming to see Evered to-night," he said. "I want to board at the farm while I work on these pictures—that is, I want permission to camp down here by the swamp somewhere, and get milk and eggs and things from you. Do you think I can?"

"Camp?" she echoed.

"Yes."

She looked round curiously, as though she expected to see his equipment there. "Haven't you a tent?"

He laughed. "No. I've a tarp for a shelter; and I can cut some hemlock boughs and build a shack; if you'll let me trespass."

"You could sleep in the barn I guess," she said. "Or maybe in the house."

He shook his head. "No roof for mine. This is my vacation, you understand. I can sleep under a roof at home."

"You'll be getting wet all the time."

"I'll dry when the sun comes out."

She asked, "Who's going to cook for you?"

"I'm a famous cook," he told her.

She had the rooted distrust of the open air which is common among the people of the farms. She could not see why a man should sleep on the ground when he might have hay or a bed; and she could not believe in the practicality of cooking over an open fire; especially when there was a stove at hand.

"You'll have to see Mr. Evered," she said uneasily.

So it happened that they two went back through the swamp together and up the hill; and they came side by side to meet Evered and John in the barnyard by the kitchen door.

They had their colloquy there in the open barnyard, while the slanting rays of the sun drew lengthening shadows from where they stood. Darrin spoke to Evered. John went into the house after a moment and built a fire for Ruth; and then he came out again while the girl went about the business of supper.

Darrin was a good talker; and Evered's silence made him seem like a good listener. When John came out he was able to tell Darrin something of the moose in the swamp, their haunts and their habits. Darrin listened as eagerly as he had talked. He told them at last what he had come to do; he explained how by trigger strings and hidden cameras and flash-light powders he hoped to capture the images of the shy giants of the forest. John listened with shining eyes. The project was of a sort to appeal to him. As for Evered, he had little to say, smoked stolidly, stared out across his fields. The sunlight on his hair accentuated the white streaks in it, and John looking toward him once thought he had never seen his father look so old.

When Darrin put forward his request for permission to camp in the woodlot near the swamp, Evered swung his heavy head round and gave the other man his whole attention for a space. It was John's turn for silence now. He expected Evered to refuse, perhaps abusively. Evered had never liked trespassers. He said they scared his cows, trampled his hay, stole his garden stuff or his apples. But Evered listened now with a certain patience, watching Darrin; and Darrin with a nimble tongue talked on and made explanations and promises.

In the end Evered asked, "Where is it your mind to camp?"

"I've picked no place. I'll find a likely spot."

"You could sleep in the barn," said Evered, as Ruth had said before him; and Darrin laughed.

"As a matter of fact," he explained, "half the sport of this for me is in sleeping out of doors on the ground. I'm on vacation, you know. Other men like hunting, and so do I; but mine is a somewhat different kind, that's all. I won't bother you; you'll not see much of me, for I'll be about the swamp at all hours of the night, and I'll sleep a good deal in the day. You'll hardly know I'm there. Of course, I don't want to urge you against your will."

Evered's lips flickered into what might have passed for a smile. "I'm not often moved against my will," he said. "But I've no objection to your sleeping in my ground. If you keep out of the uncut hay."

"I will."

"And put out your fires. I don't want to be burned up."

Darrin laughed. "I'm not a novice at this, Mr. Evered," he said. "You'll not have to kick me off."

Evered nodded; and John said, "You want to keep out of the bull's pasture too. You'll know it. There's a high wire fence round."

Darrin said soberly, "I've heard of the red bull."

"He killed my wife," said Evered; and there was something so stark in the bald statement that it shocked and silenced them. Evered himself flushed when he had spoken, as though his utterance had been unconsidered, had burst from his overfull heart.

"I know," Darrin told him.

John said after a moment's silence, "If there's any way I can help—I know the swamp. As much as any man. And I've seen the moose in there."

There was a certain eagerness in his voice; and Darrin said readily, "Of course. I'd like it."

He said he would tramp to town and come with his gear next morning. John offered to drive him over, but he shook his head. As he started away Ruth came to the kitchen door, and he looked toward her, and she said hesitantly, "Don't you want to stay to supper?"

He thanked her, shook his head. Evered and John in the barnyard watched him go; and Evered saw Ruth leave the kitchen door and move to a window from which she could see him go up the lane toward the main road.

Evered asked John: "What do you make of him?"

"I like him," said John. "I'm—glad you let him stay."

"Know why I let him stay?"

"Why—no."

"See him and Ruth together? See her watching him?"

"I didn't notice."

Evered's lips twitched in the nearest approach to mirth he ever permitted himself. "Ought to have better eyes, John; if you're minded to keep hold o' Ruth. She likes him. If I'd swore at him, shipped him off, she'd have been all on his side from the start."

John, a little troubled, shook his head. "Ruth's all right," he said. "Give her time."

Evered said, that wistful note in his voice plain for any man to hear, "I don't want Ruth leaving us. So I let Darrin stay."

# CHAPTER XI

DARRIN came to the farm. He made his camp by the spring where Mary Evered had loved to sit, and where she had been killed. John knew this at the time, was on the spot when Darrin built his fireplace in a bank of earth, waist high, and watched the other shape hemlock boughs into a rain-shedding shelter.

He did not remonstrate; but he did say, "Shouldn't think you'd want to sleep here."

Darrin looked at him curiously; and he laughed a little.

"You mean—the red bull?" he asked. And when John nodded he said, "Oh, I'm not afraid of ghosts. The world's full of ghosts." There was a sudden hardness in his eye. "I'm a sort of a ghost myself, in a way."

John wondered what he meant; but he was not given to much questioning, and did not ask. Nevertheless, Darrin's word stayed hauntingly in his mind.

He told Ruth where Darrin was camping; and the girl listened thoughtfully, but made no comment. John knew that Ruth was accustomed to go to the spring now and then, as her sister had done. He wondered whether she would go there now. There was no jealousy in John; his heart was not built for it. Nevertheless, there was a deep concern for Ruth, deeper than he had any way of expressing. The matter worried him a little.

They did not speak of Darrin's camping place to Evered, and Evered asked no questions. Darrin came to the house occasionally for supplies, but it happened that he did not encounter Evered at such times. He was always careful to ask for the man, to leave some word of greeting for him; and once he bade them tell Evered to come down and see his camp. They did not do so. Some instinct, unspoken and unacknowledged, impelled both Ruth and John to keep Evered and Darrin apart. Neither was conscious of this feeling, yet both were moved by it.

John, prompted to some extent by his father's warning, had begun in an awkward fashion to seek to please Ruth and to win back favor in her eyes. He felt himself uneasy and at a loss in the presence of Darrin, felt himself at a disadvantage in any contest with the other. John was a man of the country, of the farm, and he had grace to know it. Darrin had the ease of one who has rubbed shoulders with many men in many places; he was not confused in Ruth's presence; he was rather at his best when she was near, while John was ill at ease and words came hard to him. Darrin took care to be friendly with them both; and he and John on more than one night drove deep into the swamp together on Darrin's quest. John, busy about the farm, was unable to join Darrin in the daytime; but the other scoured through the marsh for tracks and traces, and then enlisted John to help him move cameras into position, lay flash-powder traps, or stalk the moose at their feeding in desperate attempts at camera snap-shooting.

Sometimes, in the afternoons, John knew that Ruth went down to the spring and talked with Darrin. Darrin told her of his ventures in the swamp; and she told Darrin in her turn the story of the tragedy that had been enacted here by the spring where he was camping. John, crossing the woodlot on some errand, came upon them there one afternoon, and passed by on the knoll above them without having been seen. The picture they made remained with him and troubled him.

When Darrin had been some ten days on the farm and September was coming in with a full moon in the skies it happened one night that Evered drove to Fraternity for the mail and left John and Ruth alone together. When she had done with the dishes she came out to find him on the door-step, smoking in the moonlight; and she stood above him for a moment, till he looked up at her with some question in his eyes.

She asked then, "Are you going into the swamp with Mr. Darrin to-night?"

He said, "No. He's out of plates. There's some due to-morrow; and he's waiting."

She was silent a moment longer, then said swiftly, as though anxious to be rid of the words, "Let's go down and see him."

If John was hurt or sorry he made no sign. He got to his feet. "Why, all right," he said. "It's bright. We'll not need a lantern."

As they moved across the barnyard to the bars and entered the woodlot the girl began to talk, in a swift low voice, as though to cover some unadmitted embarrassment. A wiser man might have been disturbed; but John was not analytical, and so he enjoyed it. It was the first time they had talked together at any length since Mary died. It was, he thought, like the old happy times. He felt warmed and comforted and happier than he had been for many weeks past. She was like the old Ruth again, he told himself.

Darrin was glad to see them. He built up his fire and made a place for Ruth to sit upon his blankets, leaning against a bowlder, and offered John cigars. The man knew how to play host, knew how to be interesting. John saw Ruth laugh wholeheartedly for the first time in months. He thought she was never so lovely as laughing.

When they went back up the hill together she fell silent and sober again; and he looked down and saw her eyes, clear in the moonlight. Abruptly, without knowing what he did, he put his arm round her; and for an instant she seemed to yield to him, so that he drew her toward him as he was used to do. He would have kissed her.

She broke away and cried out: "No, no, no! I told you no, John."

He said gently, "I think a lot of you, Ruth."

She shook her head, backing away from him; and he heard the angry note creep back into her voice. "You mustn't, ever," she told him. "Oh, can't you understand?"

Some hot strain in the man came to the surface; he cried with an eloquence that was strange on his slow lips, "I love you. That's all I understand. I always will. You've got to know that too. You———"

She said, "Hush! I won't listen. You—you're your father over. He's not content but he master everyone and every thing; master everyone about him. Break them. Master his beasts and his wife. You're his own son. You're an Evered." Her hands were tightening into fists at her side. "Oh, you would want to boss me the way he——— I won't, I won't! You shan't—shan't ever do it."

"I'll be kind to you," he said.

There was a softer note in her voice. "John, John," she told him. "I'm sorry. I did love you. I tried to shut my eyes. I tried to pretend that Mary was happy with him. You're like him. I thought I'd be happy with you. She told me one day how he used be. It frightened me, because he was like you. But I did love you, John. Till Mary died. Then I knew. He'd killed her. He made her want to die. And he had driven that great bull into a killing thing—by the way he treated it.

"Oh, I've seen your father clear, John. I know what he is. You're like him. I couldn't ever love you."

He said in a hot quick tone—because she was very lovely—that she would love him, must, some day; and she shook her head.

"Don't you see?" she told him. "You're trying already to make me do what you want. Oh, John, can't you Evereds see any living thing without crushing it? Mr. Darrin———" She caught herself, went on. "See how different he is. He goes into the swamp, and he has to be a thousand times more careful, more crafty than you when you hunt. But you come home with a bloody ugly thing across your shoulders; and he comes with a lovely picture, that will always be beautiful, and that so many people will see. He outwits the animals; he proves himself against them. But he doesn't kill them to do it, John. You—your father——— Oh, can't you ever see?"

His thoughts were not quick enough to cope with her; but he said awkwardly, "I'm not—always killing things. I've left many a trout go that I might have killed. And deer too."

"Because it's the law," she said harshly. "But it's in you to kill—crush and bruise and destroy. Don't you see the difference? You don't have to beat a thing, a beast, to make it yield to you. You Evereds."

"I'm not a horse beater," he said.

"It's the blood of you," she told him. "You will be."

"There's some times," he suggested, "when you've got to be hard."

"I've heard your father say that very thing."

They were moving slowly homeward now, speaking brokenly, with longer silences between. The night was almost as bright as day, the moon in midheavens above them. Ahead the barn and the house bulked large, casting dark shadows narrowly along their foundation walls. There was a fragrance of the hayfields in the air. The rake itself lay a little at one side as they came into the barnyard, its spindling curved tines making it look not unlike a spider crouching there. The bars rattled when John lowered them for her to pass through; and the red bull in the barn heard the sound and snorted sullenly at them.

John said to her, "You'd be having a man handle that bull by kindness, maybe."

She swung about and said quickly, "I'd be having a man take an ax and chop that red bull to little bits."

He stood still and she looked up at him; and after an instant she hotly asked, "Are you laughing? Why are you laughing at me?"

He said gently, "You that were so strong against any killing—talking so of the red bull."

She cried furiously, "Oh, you—— John Evered, you! I hate you! I'll always hate you. You and your father—both of you. Don't you laugh at me!"

A little frightened at the storm he had evoked he touched her arm. She wrenched violently away, was near falling, recovered herself. "Don't touch me!" she bade him.

He watched her run into the house.

# CHAPTER XII

ONE day in the first week of September, a day when there was a touch of frost in the air, and a hurrying and scurrying of the clouds overhead as though they would escape the grip of coming winter, Evered took down his double-bitted ax from its place in the woodshed and went to the grindstone and worked the two blades to razor edge. John was in the orchard picking those apples which were already fit for harvesting. Ruth was helping him.

There was not much of the fruit, and Evered had said to them, "I'll go down into the woodlot and get out some wood."

When he was gone Ruth and John looked at each other; and John asked, "Does he know Darrin is there, I wonder? Know where he is?"

Ruth said, "I don't know. He sees more than you think. Anyway, it won't hurt him to know."

Evered shaped the ax to his liking, slung it across his shoulder, and walked down the wood road till he came to a growth of birch which was ready for the ax. The trees would be felled and cut into lengths where they lay, then hauled to the farm and piled in the shed to season under cover for a full twelve months before it was time to use the wood. Evered's purpose now was simply to cut down the trees, leaving the later processes for another day.

He had chosen the task in response to some inner uneasiness which demanded an outlet. The man's overflowing energy had always been his master; it drove him now, drove him with a new spur—the spur of his own thoughts. He could never escape from them; he scarce wished to escape, for he was never one to dodge an issue. But if he had wished to forget, Fraternity would not have permitted it. The men of the town, he saw, were watching him with furtive eyes; the women looked upon him spitefully. He knew that most people thought he should have killed the red bull before this; but Evered would not kill the bull, partly from native stubbornness, partly from an unformed feeling that he, not the bull, was actually responsible. He was growing old through much thought upon the matter; and it is probable that only his own honest certainty of his wife's misdoing kept him from going mad. He slept little. His nerves tortured him.

He struck the ax into the first tree with a hot energy that made him breathe deep with satisfaction. He sank the blade on one side of the tree, and then on the other, and the four-inch birch swayed and toppled and fell. The man went furiously to the next, and to the next thereafter. The sweat began to bead his forehead and his pulses began to pound.

He worked at a relentless pace for perhaps half an hour, drunk with his own labors. At the end of that time, pausing to draw breath, he knew that he was thirsty. It was this which first brought the spring to his mind, the spring where his wife had died.

He had not been near the spot since the day he found her there. The avoidance had been instinctive rather than conscious. He hated the place and in some measure he feared it, as much as it was in the man to fear anything. He could see it all too vividly without bringing the actual surroundings before his eyes. The thought of it tormented him. And when his thirst made him remember the spring now his first impulse was to avoid it. His second—because it was ever the nature of the man to meet danger or misfortune or unpleasantness face to face—was to go to the place and drink his fill. He stuck his ax into a stump and started down the hill. This was not like that other day when he had gone along this way. That day his wife had been killed was sultry and lowering and oppressive; there was death in the very air. Today was bright, crisp, cool; the air like wine, the earth a vivid panorama of brilliant coloring, the sky a vast blue canvas with white clouds limned lightly here and there. A day when life quickened in the veins; a day to make a man sing if there was song in him.

There was no song in Evered; nevertheless, he felt the influence of the glory all about him. It made him, somehow, lonely; and this was strange in a man so used to loneliness. It made him unhappy and a little sorry for himself, a little wistful. He wanted, without knowing it, someone to give him comradeship and sympathy and friendliness. He had never realized before how terribly alone he was.

His feet took unconsciously the way they had taken on that other day; but his thoughts were not on the matter, and so he came at last to the knoll above the spring with something like a shock of surprise, for he saw a man sitting below; and for a moment it seemed to him this man was Semler, that Mary sat beside him. He brushed a rough hand across his eyes, and saw that what he had taken for his wife's figure was just a roll of blanket laid across a rock; and he saw that the man was not Semler but Darrin.

He had never thought of the possibility that Darrin might have camped beside the spring. Yet it was natural enough. This was the best water anywhere along the swamp's edge. A man might drink from the brook, but not with satisfaction in a summer of such drought as this had seen. But the spring had a steady flow of cool clear water in the driest seasons. This was the best place for a camp. Darrin was here.

Evered stood still, looking down on Darrin's camp, until the other man felt his eyes and looked up and saw him.

When he saw Evered, Darrin got to his feet and laid aside his book and called cheerfully, "Come aboard, sir. Time you paid me a call."

Evered hesitated; then he went, stumbling a little, down to where Darrin was. "I'm getting out some wood," he said. "I just came down for a drink."

"Sit down," said Darrin in a friendly way. "Fill your pipe."

The old Evered, the normal Evered even now would have shaken his head, bent for his drink from the spring and gone back to his work. But Evered was in want of company this day; and Darrin had a cheerful voice, a comradely eye. Darrin seemed glad to see him. Also the little hollow about the spring had a fascination for Evered. Having come to the spot he was unwilling to leave it, not because he wished to stay, but because he wished to go. He stayed because he dreaded to stay. He took Darrin's cup and dipped it in the spring and drank; and then at Darrin's insistence he sat down against the bowlder and whittled a fill for his pipe and set it going.

Darrin during this time had been talking with the nimble wit which was characteristic of the man. He made Evered feel more assured, more comfortable than he had felt for a long time. And while Darrin talked Evered's slow eyes were moving all about, marking each spot in the tragedy that was forever engraved upon his mind—there had sat his wife, there Semler, yonder stood the bull—terribly vivid, terribly real, so that the sweat burst out upon his forehead again.

Darrin, watching, asked, "What's wrong? You look troubled."

And Evered hesitated, then said huskily, "It's the first time I've been here."

He did not explain; but Darrin understood. "Since your wife was killed?"

"Yes."

Darrin nodded. "It was here by the spring, wasn't it?"

Evered answered slowly, "Yes. She was—lying over there when I found her." He pointed to the spot.

Darrin looked that way; and after a moment, eyes upon the curling smoke of his pipe, he asked casually, "Where was Semler?"

His tone was easy, mildly interested and that was all; nevertheless, his word came to Evered with an abrupt and startling force. Semler? He had told no one save John that Semler was here that day; he knew John would never have told. Ruth knew; but she too was close-mouthed. Fraternity did not know. Yet Darrin knew.

"Where was Semler?" Darrin had asked, so casually.

And Evered cried, "Semler? Who said he was here?"

Darrin looked surprised. "Why, I did not know it was a secret. He told me—himself."

Evered was tense and still where he sat. "He—you know him?"

Darrin laughed a little. "I wouldn't say that. I don't care for the man. I met him a little before I came up here, and told him where I was coming; and he advised me not to come. Told me of this—tragedy."

"Told you he was here?"

Darrin nodded. "Yes; how he tried to fight off the bull."

Evered came to his feet, half crouching. "The black liar and coward ran like a rabbit," he said under his breath; and his face was an ugly thing to see.

Darrin cried, "I'm sorry. I didn't mean to—waken old sorrows. It doesn't matter. Forget it." He sought, palpably, to change to another topic. "Are you getting in your apples yet?"

Evered would not be put off. "See here," he said. "What did Dane Semler tell you?"

"I've forgotten," said Darrin. He smiled cheerfully. "That is to say, I mean to forget. It's not my affair. Let's not talk about it."

Over Evered swept then one of those impulses to speech, akin to the impulses of confession. He exclaimed with a tragic and miserable note in his voice. "By God, if I don't talk about it sometime it'll kill me."

Darrin looked up at him, gently offered; "I'll listen, then. It may ease you to—tell the story over. Go ahead, Mr. Evered. Sit down."

Evered did not sit down. But the story burst from him. Something, Darrin's sympathy or the anger Darrin's reference to Semler had roused, touched hidden springs within the man. He spoke swiftly, eagerly, as though with a pathetic desire to justify himself. He moved to and fro, pointing, illustrating.

He told how Zeke Pitkin had brought word that the red bull was loose in the woodlot. "I stopped at the house," he said. "There was no one there; and that scared me. When I came down this way I thought of this spring. My wife used to like to come here. And I was scared, Darrin. I loved Mary Evered, Darrin."

He caught himself, as though his words sounded strangely even in his own ears. When he went on his voice was harsh and hard.

"I came to the knoll up there"—he pointed to the spot—"and saw Mary and Semler here, sitting together, talking together. Damn him! Like sweethearts!" The red floods swept across the man's face as the tide of that old rage overwhelmed him. "Damn Semler!" he cried. "Let him come hereabouts again!"

He went on after a moment: "I was too late to do anything but shout to them. The bull was coming at them from over there, head down. When I shouted they heard me, and forgot each other; and then they saw the red bull. Semler could have stopped him or turned him if he'd been a man. If I had been nearer I could have killed the beast with my hands, in time. But I was too far away; and Semler ran. I tell you, Darrin, he ran! He turned tail, and squawked, and ran along the hillside there. But Mary did not run. She could not; or she wouldn't. And the red bull hit her here; and tossed her there. One blow and toss. He has no horns, you'll mind. Semler running, all the time. Tell him, when you go back—tell him he lied."

He was abruptly silent, his old habit of reticence upon him. And he was instantly sorry that he had spoken at all. To speak had been relief, had somehow eased him. Yet who was Darrin? Why should he tell this man?

Darrin said gently, "The bull did not trample her?"

Evered answered curtly, "No. I reached him."

Darrin nodded. "You could handle him?"

"The beast knows me," said Evered.

And even while he spoke he remembered how the great bull, as though regretting that which he had done, had stood quietly by until he was led away. He did not tell Darrin this; there were no more words in him. He had spoken too much already. Darrin was watching him now, he saw; and it seemed to Evered that there was a hard and hostile light of calculation in the other's eye.

He turned away his head, and Darrin asked, "How came she here with Semler?"

Evered swung toward the man so hotly that for a moment Darrin was afraid; and then the older man's eyes misted and his lips twisted weakly and he brushed them with the back of his hand.

He did not answer Darrin at all; and after a moment Darrin said, "Forgive me. It must hurt you to remember; to look round here. You must see the whole thing over again."

Evered stood still for a moment; then he said abruptly: "I've sat too long. I'll be back at work."

He went stiffly up the knoll. Darrin called after him, "Come down again. You know the way."

Evered did not turn, he made no reply. When he was beyond the other's sight he stopped once and looked back, and his eyes were faintly furtive. He muttered something under his breath. He was cursing his folly in having talked with Darrin.

Back at his work Evered was uneasy; but his disquiet would have been increased if he could have seen how Darrin busied himself when he was left alone. The man sat still where he was till Evered had passed out of sight above the knoll; sat still with thoughtful eyes, studying the ground about him and considering the things which Evered had said. And once while he sat with his eyes straight before him, thinking on Evered's words, he said to himself: "The man did love his wife." And again: "There's something hurting him."

After a little he got up and climbed the knoll cautiously, till he could look in the direction Evered had taken. Evered was not in sight; and when he could be sure of this Darrin went along the shelf above the spring, toward the wood road that came down from the farm. At the road he turned round and retraced his steps, trying to guess the path Evered would have taken to come in sight of the spring itself.

When he came to the edge of the knoll he noted the spot, and cast back and tried again, and still again. He seemed to seek the farthest spot from which the spring was visible. When he had chosen this spot he stood still, surveying the land below, picturing to himself the tragedy that had been enacted there.

He seemed to come to some conclusion in the end, for he paced with careful steps the distance from where he stood to the rock where Mary Evered had been sitting. From that spot again he paced the distance to the alder growth through which the bull had come. Returning, eyes thoughtful, he took pencil and paper and plotted the scene round him, and set dots upon it to mark where Evered must have stood, and where Mary and Semler had sat, and the way by which the bull had come.

The man sat for a long hour that afternoon with this rude map before him, considering it; and he set down distances upon it, and marked the trees. Once he took pebbles and moved them upon his map as the bull and Semler and Evered must have moved upon this ground.

In the end, indecision in his eyes, he folded the paper and put it carefully into his pocket. Then he made a little cooking fire and prepared his supper and ate it. When he had cleaned up his camp he put on coat and cap and started along the hillside below the bull pasture to the road that led toward Fraternity.

This was not unusual with Darrin. He was accustomed to go to the village three or four times a week for his mail or to sit round the stove in Will Bissel's store and listen to the talk of the country. He had got some profit from this: Jim Saladine, for example, told him one night of a fox den, and took him next day to the spot; and by a week's patience Darrin had been able to get good pictures of the little foxes at their play. And Jean Bubier had taken him up to the head of the pond to see a cow moose pasturing with Jean's own cows. Besides these tangible pieces of fortune he had acquired a fund of tales of the woods. He liked the talk about the stove, and took his own share in it so modestly that the men liked him.

Once or twice during his stay in the town there had been talk of Evered; and Darrin had led them to tell the man's deeds. Great store of these tales, for Evered's daily life had an epic quality about it. From the murdering red bull the stories went back and back to that old matter of the knife and Dave Riggs, now years agone. Telling this story Lee Motley told Darrin one night that it had made a change in Evered.

Darrin had asked, "What did he do?"

And Motley said: "First off, he didn't seem bothered much. But it changed him. He'd been wild and strong and hard before, but there was some laughing in him. I've always figured he took the thing hard. I've not seen the man laugh, right out, since then."

Darrin said, "You can't blame him. It's no joke to kill a man."

Motley nodded his agreement. "It made a big change in Evered," he repeated.

Darrin's interest in Evered had not been sufficiently marked to attract attention, for Evered was a figure of interest to all the countryside. Furthermore, there was talk that Darrin and Ruth MacLure liked each other well; and the town thought it natural that Darrin should be curious as to the man who might be his brother-in-law. Everyone knew that Ruth and John Evered had been more than friends. There was a friendly and curious interest in what looked like a contest between Darrin and John.

This night at Will's store Darrin had little to say. He bought paper and envelopes from Will and wrote two letters at the desk in Will's office; and he mailed them, with a special-delivery stamp upon each one. That was a thing not often done in Fraternity; and Will noticed the addresses upon the letters. To Boston men, both of them.

Afterward, Darrin sat about the store for a while, and then set off along the road toward Evered's farm. Zeke Pitkin gave him a lift for a way; and Darrin remembered that Evered had named this man, and he said to Zeke: "You saw Evered's bull break out, that day the beast killed Mary Evered, didn't you?"

Zeke said yes; and he told the tale, coloring it with the glamor of tragedy which it would always have in his eyes. And he told Darrin—though Darrin had heard this more than once before—how Evered had killed his, Zeke's, bull with a knife thrust in the neck, a day or two before the tragedy. "That same heavy knife of his," he said. "The one he killed Dave Riggs with."

Darrin asked, "Still uses it—to butcher with?"

"Yes, sir," said Zeke. "I've seen him stick more'n one pig with that old knife in the last ten year."

Darrin laughed a little harshly. "Not very sentimental, is he?"

"There ain't a human feeling in the man," Pitkin declared.

When Zeke stopped to let Darrin down at the fork of the road Darrin asked another question. "Funny that Semler should skip out so sudden that day, wasn't it?"

"You bet it uz funny," Zeke agreed. "I've allus said it was."

"Did you see him the day he left?"

Pitkin shook his head. "Huh-uh. I was busy all day, and over in North Fraternity in the aft'noon. Got to the store right after he lit out."

Darrin walked to his camp, lighting his steps with an electric torch, and made a little fire for cheerfulness' sake, and wrapped in his blankets for sleep. He had set a camera in the swamp that day, with a string attached to the shutter in a fashion that should give results if a moose came by. He wondered whether luck would be with him. His thoughts as sleep crept on him shifted back to Evered again. A puzzle there—a question of character, of reaction to emotional stimulus. He asked himself: "Now if I were an emotional, hot-tempered man and came upon my wife with another man, and saw her in swift peril of her life—what would I do?"

He was still wondering, still questioning, still trying to put himself in Evered's shoes when at last he dropped asleep.

# CHAPTER XIII

DARRIN and Ruth had come to that point in friendship where they could sit silently together, each busy with his or her own thoughts, without embarrassment. The girl liked to come down the hill of an afternoon for an hour with the man; and sometimes he read to her from one of the books of which he had a store. And sometimes he showed her the pictures he had made—strange glimpses of the life of the swamp. His camera trap caught curious scenes. Now and then a deer, occasionally a moose, once a wildcat screeching in the night. And again they had to look closely to see what it was that had tugged the trigger string; and sometimes it was a rabbit, and sometimes it was a mink; and at other times it was nothing at all that they could discover in the finished photograph. Once a great owl dropped on some prey upon the ground and touched the string; and the plate caught him, wings flying, talons reaching—a picture of the wild things that prey.

Most of the pictures were imperfect—blurred or shadowed or ill-focused. Out of them all there were only four or five that Darrin counted worth the saving; but he and Ruth found fascination in the study of even the worthless ones.

It was inevitable that the confidence between them should develop swiftly in these afternoons together. It was not surprising that Ruth one afternoon dared ask Darrin a question. She had been curiously silent, studying him, until he noticed it, and laughed at her for it; and she told him then, "I'm wondering—whether we really know you here."

He looked at her with a quick intentness, smiled a little. "Why?" he asked. "What are you thinking?"

She shook her head. "I don't know, exactly. Just that sometimes I felt you're hiding something; that you're not thinking about the things you—seem to think about."

He said good-naturedly, "You're making a mystery out of me."

"A little," she admitted.

"There's no mystery," he said; and he added softly: "There's a deal more mystery about you, to me."

He had never, as they say, made love to her. Yet there was that in his tone now which made her flush softly and look away from him. Watching her he hesitated. His hand touched hers. She drew her hand away and rose abruptly.

"I must go back to the house," she said. "It's time I was starting supper."

He was on his feet, facing her; but there was only cheerful friendliness in his eyes. He would not alarm her. "Come again," he said. "I like to have you come."

"You never come to the house, except for eggs and things. You ought to come and see us."

"Perhaps I will," he said; and he watched her as she climbed the knoll and disappeared. His eyes were very gentle; there would have been in them an exultant light if he could have seen the girl, once out of his sight, stop and look back to where the smoke of his little fire rose above the trees.

Darrin was much in her thoughts during these days. She would have thought of him more if she had been able to think less of John.

# CHAPTER XIV

DARRIN'S departure came abruptly. He had gone to the village one night for his mail, and found a letter waiting, which he read with avid eyes. Having read it he put it away in his pocket, and came to Will Bissell and asked how he might most quickly reach Boston.

Will told him there was a morning train from town; and Darrin nodded and left the store. He decided to walk the ten miles through the night. It was cool and clear; the walk would be good for him. It would give him time for thinking.

He went back to his camp and slept till three in the morning. Then he made a little breakfast and ate it and packed his camp belongings under his tarpaulin for cover. To the tarp he fastened a note, addressed to Ruth. He wrote simply:

"*Dear Ruth*: I have to go away for four or five days, hurriedly. I would have said goodby if there were time. If it rains will you ask John to put my things under shelter somewhere? In the barn will do. There is a camera set at the crossing of the brook where the old pine is down. Perhaps he will find that and take care of it for me. My other things in the box here are safe enough. The box is waterproof.

"I will not be long gone. I'm taking the morning train from town. Please remember me to Mr. Evered.

"Yours, FRED."

At a little after four, dressed in tramping clothes, but with other garments in a bundle under his arm, he started for town. He had time to change his garments there, and cash a check at the bank, and have a more substantial breakfast before he boarded the morning train.

Ruth discovered that Darrin had gone on the afternoon of his going. She went down to his camp by the spring with an eagerness of anticipation which she did not admit even to herself; and when she saw that he was not there she was at once relieved and unhappy.

The girl had stopped on the knoll above the camp; and she stood there for a moment looking all about, thinking Darrin might be somewhere near. Then she marked the careful order of the spot, and saw that all the camp gear was stowed away; and abruptly she guessed what had happened. She ran then down the knoll, and so came almost at once upon the note he had left for her.

She read this through, frowning and puzzling a little over the intricacies of his handwriting; and she did not know whether to be unhappy over his going or happy that he had remembered to leave this word for her. She did not press the scribbled note against her bosom, but she did read it through a second time, and then refold it carefully, and then take it out and read it yet again. In the end it was still in her hand when she turned reluctantly back up the hill. She put it in the top drawer of her bureau in her room.

She told John and Evered at suppertime that Darrin was gone. Evered seemed like a man relieved of a burden, till she added, "He's coming back again, though."

John asked, "How do you know?"

"He left a note for me," she said.

John bent over his plate, hiding the hurt in his eyes. The girl told him of the camera set in the swamp, and John promised to go and fetch it, and to bring Darrin's other belongings under shelter in the woodshed or the barn.

He managed this the next day; and Ruth made occasion to go to the barn more than once for the sheer happiness of looking upon them. John caught her at it once; but he did not let her know that he had seen. The young man was in these days woefully unhappy.

It is fair to say that he had reason to be. Ruth was kind to him, never spoke harshly or in an unfriendly fashion; in fact, she was almost too friendly. There was a finality about her friendliness which baffled him and erected a barrier between him and her. The man tried awkwardly to bring matters back to the old sweet footing between them; but the girl was of nimbler wit than he. She put him off without seeming to do so; she erected an impassable defense about herself.

On the surface they were as they had always been. Evered could see no difference in their bearing. Neighbors who occasionally stopped at the house decided that John and Ruth were going to be married when the time should come; and they told each other they had always said so. Before others the relations between the two were pleasantly friendly; but there were no longer the sweet stolen moments when their arms entwined and their lips met. When they were alone together Ruth treated John as though others were about; and John knew no way to break through her barriers.

About the fifth day after Darrin's going Ruth began to expect his return. He did not come on that day, nor on the next, nor on the next thereafter. She became a little wistful, a little lonely. Toward the middle of the second week she found herself clinging with a desperate earnestness to a despairing hope. He had promised to come back; she thought he would come back. There had never been any word of more than friendliness between them; yet the girl felt that such a word must come, and that he would return to speak it.

One night she dreamed that he would never come again, and woke to find tears streaming across her cheeks. She lay awake for a long time, eyes wide and staring, wondering if she loved him.

During this interval of Darrin's absence there manifested itself in Evered a curious wistful desire to placate Ruth; to win her good will.

She noticed it first one day when the man had been very still, sitting all day in the kitchen with his eyes before him, brooding over unguessed matters. It was a day of blustering, blowing rain, a day when the wind lashed about the house and there was little that could be done out of doors. Ruth, busy about the room, watched Evered covertly; her eyes strayed toward him now and again.

She had not fully realized till that day how much the man was aging. The change had come gradually, but it had been marked. His hair, that had been black as coal six months before, was iron gray now; it showed glints that were snow white, here and there. The skin of his cheeks had lost its bronze luster; it seemed to have grown loose, as though the man were shrinking inside. It hung in little folds about his mouth and jaw.

His head, too, was bowing forward; his head that had always been so erect, so firm, so hard and sternly poised. His neck seemed to be weakening beneath the load it bore; and his shoulders were less square. They hung forward, as though the man were cold and were guarding his chest with his arms.

The fullness of the change came to Ruth with something of a shock, came when she was thinking it strange that Evered should be content to remain all day indoors. He was by nature an active man, of overflowing bodily energy; he was used to go out in all weathers to his tasks. She had seen him come in, dripping, in the past; his cheeks ruddy from the wet and cold, his eyes glowing with the fire of health, his chest heaving to great deep breaths of air. More and more often of late, she remembered, he had stayed near the stove and the fire, as though it comforted him.

Ruth had not John's sympathetic understanding of the heart of Evered; nevertheless, she knew, as John did, that the man had—in his harsh fashion—loved his dead wife well. She had always known this, even though she had never been able to understand how a man might hurt the woman he loved. If she had not known, she would not have blamed Evered so bitterly for all the bitter past. It was one of the counts of her indictment of him that he had indeed loved Mary; and that even so he had made the dead woman unhappy through so many years.

Watching him this day Ruth thought that sorrow was breaking him; and the thought somewhat modified, without her knowing it, the strength of her condemnation of the man. When in mid afternoon he took from her the shovel and broom with which she was preparing to clean out the ashes of the stove, and did the task himself, she was amazed and angry with herself to find in her heart a spark of pity for him.

"Let me do that, Ruthie," he had said. "It's hard for you."

He had never been a man given to small chores about the house; he was awkward at it. His very awkwardness, the earnestness of his clumsy efforts—warmed the girl's heart; she found her eyes wet as she watched him, and took recourse in an abrupt protest.

"You're spilling the ashes," she said. "Here, let me."

She would have taken the broom from him, but Evered would not let it go. He looked toward her as they held the broom between them, and there was in his eyes such an agony of desire to please her that the girl had to turn away.

What was moving in Evered's mind it is hard to say, hard to put in words. He had not yet surrendered to regret for the thing he had done; he was still able to bolster his courage, to strengthen himself by the reflection that his wife had wronged him. He was still able to fan to life the embers of his rage against her and against Semler. Yet the man was finding it hard to endure the hatred in Ruth's eyes, the silent glances which met him when he went abroad, the ostracism of the village. He wanted comradeship in these days as he had never wanted it before. He desired the friendship of mankind; he desired, in an unformed way, the affection of Ruth. The girl had come to symbolize in his thoughts something like his own conscience. He was uncertainly conscious that if she forgave him, looked kindly upon him, bore him no more malice, he might altogether forgive himself for that which he had done.

Yet when he put this thought in words it evoked a revolt in his own heart; and he would cry out to himself, "I need no forgiveness! I've nothing to forgive! I was right to let the bull.... She was false as a witch; false as hell!"

He found poor comfort in this thought. So long as he believed his wife was guilty he could endure the torment of his own remorse, could relieve the pain of it. And if Ruth would only smile upon him, be her old friendly self to him again....

The man's attentions to her were almost like an uncouth wooing. He began to study the girl's wants, to find little ways to help her, to anticipate her desires, to ease her work about the house. He sought opportunities to talk with her, and drove himself to speak gently and ingratiatingly. He called her Ruthie, though she had always been Ruth to him before.

The man was pitiful; the girl could not wholly harden her heart against him. Naturally generous and kindly she caught herself thinking that after all he had loved Mary well; that he missed her terribly. Once or twice hearing him move about his room in the night she guessed his loneliness. She was more and more sorry for Evered.

Ruth was not the only one who saw that the man was growing old too swiftly. They marked the fact at Will Bissell's store. Will saw it, and Lee Motley saw it, and Jim Saladine; these three with a certain sympathy. Jean Bubier saw it with sardonic amusement, tinged with understanding. Old Man Varney saw it with malice; and Judd in the meanness of his soul saw it with malignant delight.

"Looking for friends now, he is," Judd exclaimed one night. "Him that was so bold before. Tried to start talk with me to-day. I turned my back on the man. I'd a mind to tell him why."

Motley and Saladine spoke of the thing together. Motley said, "I think he—thought a deal of Mary—in the man's way."

And Saladine nodded and said: "Yes. But—there's more to it than that, Lee. More than we know, I figure. Something hidden behind it all. A black thing, if the whole truth was to come out. Or so it looks to me."

Saladine was a steady, thoughtful man, and Motley respected his opinion, and thought upon the matter much thereafter; but he was to come to no conclusion.

On his farm the change in Evered manifested itself in more than one way; in no way more markedly than in his lack of energy. He left most of the chores to John; and, what was more significant, he gave over to John full care of the huge red bull. It had been Evered's delight to master that brute and bend it to his will. John and Ruth both marked that he avoided it in these later days. John had the feeding of it; he cleaned its stall; he tossed in straw for the creature's bed. The bull was beginning to know him, to know that it need not fear him. He was accustomed to go into its stall and move about the beast without precautions, speaking gently when he spoke at all.

Ruth never saw this. She seldom went near the red bull's stall. She hated the animal and dreaded it. On one occasion she did go near its pen. It was suppertime and the food was hot upon the table. She called John from the woodshed, and then came to the kitchen door to summon Evered. He was leaning against the high gate of the bull's plank-walled yard looking in at the animal. Ruth called to him to come to supper, but he did not turn. She called again, and still the man did not move.

A little alarmed, for fear he might have been suddenly stricken sick, she went swiftly across the barnyard to where he stood, and looked at him, and looked into the pen.

Evered was watching the bull; and the bull stood a dozen feet away, watching the man. There was a stillness about them both which frightened the girl; a still intentness. Neither moved; their eyes met steadily without shifting. There was no emotion in either of them. It was as though the man were probing the bull's mind, as though the bull would read the man's thoughts. They were like persons hypnotized. Ruth shivered and touched Evered's arm and shook it a little.

"Supper's ready," she said.

He turned to her with eyes still glazed from the intensity of their stare.

"Supper?" he echoed. Then remembrance came to him; and he nodded heavily and said with that wistfully ingratiating note in his voice, "Yes, Ruthie, I'm coming. Come; let's go together."

He took her arm, and she had not the hardness of heart to break away from him. They went into the house side by side.

# CHAPTER XV

IN mid-October Darrin returned afoot, as he had departed; and there was no warning of his coming. He reached the farm in the afternoon. John was in the woodlot at the time, cutting the wood into cord lengths in preparation for hauling. Evered had worked in the morning, but after dinner he sat down by the kitchen stove and remained there, in the dull apathy of thought which was becoming habitual to him. He was still there and Ruth was busy about the room when Darrin came to the door. Ruth had caught sight of him through the window; she was at the door to meet him and opened it before he knocked. She wanted to tell him how glad she was to see him; but all she could do was stand very still, her right hand at her throat, her eyes on his.

He said gently, "Well, I've come back. But it has been longer than I thought it would be."

She nodded. "Yes, it has been a long time."

There was so much of confession in her tone that the man's heart pounded and he stepped quickly toward her. But when she moved back he saw Evered within the room, watching him with dull eyes; and he caught himself and his face sobered and hardened.

"My things are here?" he asked.

"In the shed," she said. "John brought them up. I'll show you."

She stepped away and he followed her into the kitchen, toward the door that opened at one side into the shed.

She had already opened the door when Evered asked huskily, "Back, are you?"

Darrin said, "Yes." There was an indescribable note of hostility in his voice which he could not disguise.

"Won't be here long now, I figure," Evered suggested.

"I don't know," said Darrin. "I'll be here till I've done what I came to do."

Evered did not speak for a minute; then he asked, "Get them moose pictures, you mean?"

Ruth looked from one man to the other in a bewildered way, half sensing the fact that both were wary and alert.

Darrin said, "Of course."

Evered shook his head. "Dangerous business, this time o' year. The old bulls have got other things on their mind besides having their pictures took."

"I'll risk it," said Darrin.

"You've a right to," Evered told him, and turned away.

Darrin watched the man for an instant; then he followed Ruth into the shed. She showed him his dunnage, packed in a stout roll; and he lifted it by the lashing and slung it across his shoulder.

"Mr. Evered is right," she said. "The moose are dangerous—in the fall."

He touched his roll with his left hand affectionately. "I've a gun here. My pistol, you know. I'll be careful."

She urged softly, "Please do."

There was so much solicitude in her voice that Darrin was shaken by it; he slid the roll to the floor.

Then Evered came to the door that led into the shed; and he said, "I'll help you down with that stuff."

Darrin shook his head. "No need," he replied. "I can handle it."

He swung it up again across his shoulder; and Ruth opened the outer door for him. She and Evered stood together watching him cross the barnyard and lower the bars and pass through and go on his way.

When he was out of sight Ruth looked up at Evered; and the man said gently, "Glad to see him, Ruthie?"

She nodded, "I like him."

"More than you like John?" the man asked.

And she said steadily, "I like them both. But Darrin is gentle, and strong too. And you Evereds are only cruelly strong."

"I wouldn't say John was cruel," the man urged wistfully.

"He's your son," she said, the old bitterness in her voice.

And Evered nodded, as though in confession. He looked in the direction Darrin had taken.

"I wonder what he's back for," he said half to himself.

Ruth did not answer, and after a little she went back into the kitchen. She heard Evered working with his ax for a while, splitting up wood for the stove; and presently he brought in an armful and dumped it in the woodbox.

It was a thing he had done before, though John was accustomed to carry her wood for her. As he dropped the wood now Evered looked toward her, as though to make sure she had seen; he smiled in a pleading, broken way. She thanked him, a certain sympathy in her voice in spite of herself. The man was so broken; he had grown so old in so short a time.

Darrin, bound toward his old camping ground at the spring, heard John's ax in the birch growth at his left, but he did not turn aside. There was a new purpose in the man; his old pleasantly amiable demeanor had altered; his eyes were steady and hard. He reached the spring and disposed his goods, with a packet of provisions which he had brought from the village.

A little later he went back up the hill to get milk and eggs from the farm. It chanced that he found Evered in the barnyard; and Evered saw him coming, and watched him approach. They came face to face at the bars, and when Darrin had passed through he stood still, eying the other man and waiting for Evered to speak. There was a steady scrutiny in Evered's eyes, a questioning; Darrin met this questioning glance with one that told nothing. His lips set a little grimly.

Evered asked at last, "You say you came back for more pictures?"

"Yes."

"I'm wondering if you'll get what you come for."

Darrin said, "I intend to."

Evered nodded quietly. "All right," he agreed. "I don't aim to hinder."

He turned toward the barn; and as he turned Darrin saw that he had his knife slung in its leather sheath upon his hip. The sheath was deep; only the tip of the knife's haft showed. Yet Darrin's eyes fastened on this with a strange intentness, as though he were moved by a morbid curiosity at sight of the thing. The heavy knife had taken so many lives.

Darrin did not move till Evered had gone into the barn and out of sight; then the younger man turned toward the house, and knocked, and Ruth opened the door.

He asked, "Can I get milk to-night, and eggs; and have you made butter?"

She had been surprised to see him so soon again; she was a little startled, could not find words at once. But she nodded and he came into the kitchen and she shut the door behind him, for the day was cold.

"We haven't milked," she said. "It will be a little while."

Darrin, whose thoughts had been on other things, found himself suddenly swept by a sense of her loveliness. He had always known that she was beautiful, but he had held back the thought, had fought against it. Now seeing her again after so long a time he forgot everything but her. She saw the slow change in his eyes; and though she had longed for it, it frightened her.

She began to tremble, and tried to speak, but all she could say was, "Oh!"

Darrin came toward her then slowly. He had not meant to speak, yet the words came before he knew. "Ah, Ruth, I have missed you so," he said.

Her eyes were dim and soft. She was miserably happy, an anguish of happiness.

He said, "I love you so, Ruth. I love you so." And he kissed her.

The girl was swept as by a tempest. She had dreamed of this man for weeks, idealizing him, thinking him all that was fine and gentle and good. She gave herself to his kisses as though she were hungry for them. She was crying, tears were flowing down her cheeks; and at first she thought this was because she was so happy, while Darrin, half alarmed, half laughing, whispered to comfort her.

Then slowly the girl knew that she was not crying because she was so happy. She could not tell why she cried; she could not put her heart in words. It was as though she were lonely, terribly lonely. And she was angry with herself at that. How could she be lonely in his arms? In Darrin's arms, his kisses on her wet cheeks?

She could not put the thought away. While he still held her she wept for very loneliness. He could not soothe her. She scarce heard him; she put her hands against him and tried to push him away, feebly at first. She did not want to push him away; yet something made her. He held her still; his arms were like bands of iron. He was so strong, so hard. Thus close against him she seemed to feel a rigor of spirit in the man. It was as though she were pressed against a wall. He freed her. "Please," he said.

And she cried, as though to persuade herself, "Oh, I do love you! I do!"

But when he would have put his arms round her again she shrank away from him, so that he forbore. She turned quickly away to her tasks. She had time to compose herself before Evered came in, and later John. Then Darrin left with the things he had come to secure, and went down the hill in the early dusk of fall.

Ruth was thoughtful that evening; she went early to her room. She was trying desperately to understand herself. She had been drawn so strongly toward Darrin, she had found him all that she wanted a man to be. She had been miserable at his going, had longed for his return. She had wanted that which had come to pass this day. The girl was honest with herself, had always been honest with herself. She had known she loved him, longed for him.

Yet now he was returned, he loved her and his kisses only served to make her miserably lonely. She could not understand; slept, still without comprehending.

Darrin, next day, did not go into the swamp. He busied himself about the spring, producing again that sketch which he had made on the day Evered told him the story of the tragedy. He was groping for something, groping for understanding, his forehead wrinkled and his eyes were sober with thought.

After he had cooked his dinner and eaten it the man sat for a long time by the fire, tending it with little sticks, watching the flames as though he expected to find in them the answer to his riddle. Once he took from his pocket a letter, and read it soberly enough, then put it back again. And once he took fresh paper and made a new sketch of the locality about him.

He seemed at last to come to some decision. The aspect of his countenance changed subtly. He got to his feet, pacing back and forth. At about four o'clock in the afternoon he put on his coat and started up the knoll toward the farm. When he had gone some fifty yards he stopped, hesitated, and came back to his camp fire. From his kit he selected the automatic pistol, saw that it held a loaded clip, belted it on. It hung under his coat inconspicuously.

He went on his way this time without hesitation; went steadily up the hill, reached the bars about the farmyard, passed through and knocked on the kitchen door.

Ruth came to the door; he asked her abstractedly, as though she were a stranger, where Evered was. She said he was in the shed; and Darrin went there and found Evered grinding an ax. The man looked up at his coming with sober eyes. Ruth had stayed in the kitchen.

Darrin said quietly, "Evered, I want to talk to you."

Evered hesitated, studying the other. He asked, "What about?"

"A good many things," Darrin told him.

Evered laid aside the ax. "All right," he said.

"Come away from the house," Darrin suggested.

There was a certain dominant note in his voice. The old Evered would have stayed where he was; but the old Evered was dead. "Come," said Darrin; and he stepped out into the yard and Evered followed him. Darrin crossed to the bars and let them down. He and Evered passed silently through.

The men went, Darrin a little in the lead, down the hill toward the spring.

# CHAPTER XVI

THE day was cold and damp and chill, with a promise of snow in the air; one of those ugly October days when coming winter seems to sulk upon the northern hills, awaiting summer's tardy going. Clouds obscured the sky, though now and then during the morning the sun had broken through, laying a patch of light upon the earth and bringing out the nearer hills in bold relief against those that were farthest off. The wind was northeasterly, always a storm sign hereabouts. There was haste in it, and haste in the air, and haste in all the wild things that were abroad. The crows overhead flew swiftly, tumbling headlong in the racking air currents. A flock of geese passed once, high in the murk, their honking drifting faintly down to earth. The few ground birds darted from cover to cover; the late-pasturing cows had gone early to the barn. Night was coming early; an ominous blackness seemed about to shut down upon the world. The very air held threats and whispers of harm.

Evered and Darrin walked in silence down along the old wood road, through a birch clump, past some dwarfed oaks, and out into the open on the shelf above the spring.

Halfway across this shelf Darrin said "I've got some questions to ask you, Evered."

Evered did not answer. Darrin had not stopped and Evered kept pace with him.

The younger man said, "This was the way you came that day your wife was killed, wasn't it?"

Evered turned his head as though to speak, hesitated. Darrin stopped and caught his eye.

"Look here," he demanded. "You've nothing to hide in that business, have you?"

"No," said Evered mildly. He wondered why he answered the other at all; yet there was something in the younger man's bearing which he did not care to meet, something dominant and commanding, as though Darrin had a right to ask, and knew that he had this right. "No," said Evered; "nothing to hide."

And Darrin repeated his question: "Was this the way you came?"

Evered nodded. As they went on nearer the spring Darrin touched his arm. "I want you to show me where you were when you first saw them—your wife, and Semler, and the bull."

Evered made no response; but a moment later he stopped. "Here," he said. Darrin looked down toward the spring and all about them. And Evered repeated, "Here, by this rock."

The younger man nodded and passed down to the spring, with Evered beside him. Darrin sat down and motioned Evered to sit.

"What did you think, when you saw them?" he asked.

Evered's cheeks colored slowly; they turned from bronze to red, from red to purple.

Darrin prompted him: "When you saw your wife and Semler here together."

"What would you have thought?" Evered asked, his voice held steady.

Darrin nodded understanding. "You were angry?" he suggested.

Evered flung his head on one side with a fierce gesture, as though to shut out some unwelcome sight that assaulted his eyes.

Darrin, watching him acutely, waited for a little before he asked: "Where was the bull, when you saw him first?"

Evered jerked his hand toward the right. "There," he said.

Darrin got up and went in that direction, and moved to and fro, asking directions, till Evered told him he was near the spot. Darrin came back then and sat down.

"You thought she loved him?" he asked under his breath.

Evered shook his head, not in negation but as though to brush the question aside. Darrin filled his pipe and lighted it, and puffed at it in silence for a while.

"Pitkin told you the bull was loose, didn't he?" he asked at last.

"Yes."

"So you came down to get the beast?"

"Yes, I came for that."

"Expect any trouble?"

"You can always look for trouble with the red bull."

"How did you plan to handle him?"

"Brad, and nose ring."

Darrin eyed the other sharply. "Wouldn't have had much time to get hold of his nose ring if he'd charged, would you?"

"I had a gun," said Evered. "A forty-five."

"Oh," said Darrin. "You had a gun?"

Evered, a little restive, cried, "Yes, damn it, I had a gun!"

"You must have felt like shooting Semler," Darrin suggested; and Evered looked at him sidewise, a little alarmed. He seemed to put himself on guard.

Darrin got to his feet. "They were sitting by these rocks, weren't they?"

"Yes."

The younger man bent above the other. "Evered," he said, "why didn't you turn the bull from its charge?"

He saw Evered's face go white, his eyes flickering to and fro. The man came to his feet.

"There was no time!" he exclaimed.

His voice was husky and unsteady; Darrin dominated him, seemed to tower above him. There was about Evered the air of a broken man.

Darrin pointed to the knoll. "You were within half a dozen strides of them. The bull was full thirty yards away."

Evered cried, "Damn you!"

He turned abruptly, climbed the knoll. Darrin stood still till Evered was almost gone from his sight, then he shouted, "Evered!" Evered went on; and Darrin with a low exclamation leaped after him. Evered must have heard his pounding steps, but he did not turn. Darrin came up with him; he tugged his pistol from its holster and jammed it against Evered's side.

"Turn round," he said, "or I'll blow you in two."

Evered did not turn; he did not stop. Dusk had fallen upon them before this; their figures were black in the growing darkness. A pelting spray of rain swept over them, the drops like ice. Above them the hill was black against the gray western sky. Behind them and below the swamp brooded, dark and still. Surrounded by gloom and wind and rain the two moved thus a dozen paces—Evered looking straight ahead, Darrin pressing the pistol against the other's ribs.

Then Darrin leaped past the other, into Evered's path, his weapon leveled. "Stop!" he said, harshly. "You wife killer, stop, and listen to me!"

Evered came on; and Darrin in a voice that was like a scream warned him: "I'll shoot!"

Evered did not stop. There was a certain dignity about the man, a certain strength. Against it Darrin seemed to rebound helplessly. Their rôles were reversed. Where Darrin had been dominant he was now weak; where Evered had been weak he was strong. The older man came on; he was within two paces. Darrin's finger pressed the trigger—indecisively. Then Evered's great fist whipped round like light and struck Darrin's hand, and the pistol flew from his grip, end over end, and struck against a bowlder with a flash of sparks in the darkness. Darrin's hand and wrist and arm were numbed by the blow; he hugged them against his body. Evered watched him, still as still. And Darrin screamed at him in a hoarse unsteady voice his black accusation.

"You killed her!" he cried. "In that black temper of yours you let the bull have her. You're a devil on earth. Evered! You're a devil among men!"

Evered lifted his hand, silencing the man. Darrin wished to speak and dared not. There was something terrible in the other's demeanor, something terrible in his calm strength and purpose.

He said at last in set tones: "It was my right. She was guilty as hell!"

Darrin found courage to laugh. "You lie," he said. "And that's what I'm here to tell you, man. I ought to take you and give you to other men, to hang by the thick neck that holds up your evil head. But this is better, Evered. This is better. I tell you your wife, whom you killed, was as clean as snow."

When he had spoken he was afraid, for the light in Evered's eyes was the father of fear. He began to fumble in his coat in a desperate haste, not daring to look away, not daring to take his eyes from Evered's. He fumbled there, and found the letter he had read beside his fire so carefully; found it and drew it, crumpled, forth. He held it toward Evered.

"Read," he cried. "Read that, and see."

Evered took the letter quietly; and before Darrin's eyes the fury died in the other man. Over his face there crept a mask of sorrow irrevocable and profound. He said no word, but took the letter and opened it. The light was dim; he could not read till Darrin flashed his electric torch upon the page. A strange picture, in that moment, these two—Evered, the old and breaking man; Darrin, young and vigorous; Evered dominant, Darrin tremulously exultant; Evered, his great head bent, his unaccustomed eyes scanning the written lines; Darrin holding the light beside him.

Evered was slow in reading the letter, for in the first place it was written in his wife's hand, and he had loved her; so that his eyes were dimmed. He was not conscious of the words he read, though they were not important. It was the message of the lines that came home to him; the unmistakable truth that lay behind them. The letter of an unhappy woman to a man whom she had found friendly and kind. She told Semler that she loved Evered; told him this so simply there could be no questioning. Would always love Evered. Bade Semler forget her, be gone, never return. Nothing but friendliness for him. Bade him not make her unhappy. And at the end, again, she wrote that she loved Evered.

The man who had killed her did not so much read this letter as absorb it, let it sink home into his heart and carry its own conviction there.

It was not curiosity that moved him, not doubt that made him ask Darrin quietly: "How got you this?"

"From Semler," Darrin told him. "I found him—followed him half across the country—told him what I guessed. That was the only letter he ever had from her. Written the day you killed her. Damn you, do you see!"

"How came they together?"

"He knew she liked to come to the spring; he found her there, argued with her. She told him she loved you; there was no moving her. She loved you, who killed her. You devil of a man!"

Evered folded the letter carefully and put it into his coat. "Why do you tell me?" he asked.

"Because I know you cared for her!" Darrin cried. "Because I know this will hurt you worse than death itself."

Evered standing very still shook his head slowly. "That was not my meaning," he explained patiently. "That is my concern. Why did you tell me? Why so much trouble for this? How did the matter touch you, Darrin?"

The younger man had waited for this moment, waited for it through the years of his manhood. He had planned toward it for months past, shaping it to his fancy. He had looked forward to it as a moment of triumph; he had seen himself towering in just condemnation above one who trembled before him. He had been drunk with this anticipation.

But the reality was not like his dreams. He knew that Evered was broken; that his soul must be shattered. Yet he could not exult. There was such a strength of honest sorrow in the old man before him, there was so much dignity and power that Darrin in spite of himself was shamed and shaken. He felt something that was like regret. He felt himself mean and small; like a malicious, mud-slinging, inconsiderable fragment of a man. His voice was low, it was almost apologetic when he answered the other's question.

"How did the matter touch you, Darrin?" Evered asked; and the rain swept over them in a more tempestuous fusilade.

Darrin said in a husky choking voice: "I'm Dave Riggs' son. You killed my father."

Evered, silent a moment, slowly nodded as though not greatly surprised. "Dave Riggs' boy," he echoed. "Aye, I might have known." And he added: "I lost you, years agone. I tried to make matters easier for you, for Dave's sake. I was sorry for that matter, Darrin."

Darrin tried to flog his anger to white heat again. "You killed my father," he exclaimed. "When I was still a boy I swore that I'd pay you for that. And when I grew up I planned and planned. And when I heard about your wife, I came up here, to watch you—find out. I felt there was something. I told you I'd seen Semler, trapped you. You told me more than you meant to tell. And then I got trace of him, followed him. I did it to blast you, Evered; pay you for what you did to me. That's why."

He ended lamely; his anger was dead; his voice was like a plea.

Evered said gently and without anger. "It was your right." And a moment later he turned slowly and went away, up the hill and toward his home.

Darrin, left behind, labored again to wake the exultation he had counted on; but he could not. He had hungered for this revenge of his, but there is no substance in raw and naked vengeance. You cannot set your teeth in it. Darrin found that it left him empty, that he was sick of himself and of his own deeds.

"It was coming to him," he cried half aloud.

But he could not put away from his thoughts the memory of Evered's proud dignity of sorrow; he was abashed before the man.

He stumbled back to his rain-swept camp like one who has done a crime.

# CHAPTER XVII

WHEN Evered reached the farm, dark had fully fallen; and the cold rain was splattering against the buildings, driven by fierce little gusts of wind from the northwest as the direction of the storm shifted. The man walked steadily enough, his head held high. What torment was hidden behind his proud bearing no man could guess. He went to the kitchen, and Ruth told him that John must be near done with the milking. Evered nodded, as though he were tired. Ruth saw that he was wet, and when he took off his coat and hat she brought him a cup of steaming tea and made him drink it. He said, "Thanks, Ruthie!" And he took the cup from her hands and sipped it slowly, the hot liquid bringing back his strength.

His trousers were soaked through at the knees. She bade him go in and change them; and he went to his room. When John came from the barn Evered had not yet come out into the kitchen again. Supper was ready and Ruth went to his door and called to him.

He came out; and both Ruth and John saw the strange light in the man's eyes. He did not speak and they did not speak to him. There was that about him which held them silent. He ate a little, then went to his room again and shut the door. They could hear him for a little while, walking to and fro. Then the sound of his footsteps ceased.

Only one door lay between his room and the kitchen; and unconsciously the two hushed their voices, so that they might not disturb him. John got into dry clothes, then helped Ruth with the dishes, brought fresh water from the pump to fill the tank at the end of the stove, brought wood for the morning, turned the separator, and finally sat smoking while she cleaned the parts of that instrument. They spoke now and then; but there was some constraint between them. Both of them were thinking of Evered.

Ruth, her work finished, came and sat down by the stove with a basket of socks to be darned, and her needle began to move carefully to and fro in the gaping holes she stretched across her darning egg.

John asked her in a low voice, "Did you mark trouble in my father this night?"

She looked at him, concern in her eyes. "Yes. There was something. He seemed happier, somehow; yet very sad too."

He said, "His eyes were shining, like."

"I saw," she agreed.

John smoked for a little while. Then: "I'm wondering what it is," he murmured. "Something has happened to him."

Ruth, head bent above her work, remembered Darrin's coming, his summons. But she said nothing till John asked: "Do you know what it was?"

"He was talking with Fred," she said; and slowly, cheeks rosy, amended herself: "With Mr. Darrin."

John nodded. "I knew they were away together."

"Mr. Darrin came for him," said Ruth. "He took your father away."

They said no more of the matter, for there was nothing more to say; but they thought a great deal. Now and then they spoke of other things. Outside the house the wind was whistling and lashing the weatherboards with rain; and after a while the sharp sound of the raindrops was intensified to a clatter and John said, "It's turned to hail. There'll be snow by morning."

The girl thought of Darrin. "He'll be wet and cold out in this. He ought to come up to the barn."

John smiled. "He can care for himself. His shelter will turn this, easy. He'd come if he wanted to come."

His tone was friendly and Ruth asked, watching him, "You like Mr. Darrin, don't you?"

"Yes," John told her. "Yes," he said slowly; "I like the man."

What pain the words cost him he hid from her eyes altogether. She was, vaguely, a little disappointed. She had not wanted John to like Darrin; and yet she—loved the man. She must love him; she had longed for him so. Thinking of him as she sat here with her mending in her lap she felt again that unaccountable pang of loneliness. And the girl looked sidewise at John. John was watching the little flames that showed through the grate in the front of the stove. He seemed to pay no heed to her.

After a while Ruth said she would go to bed; and she put away her basket of mending, set her chair in place by the table and went to the door that led toward her own room. John, still sitting by the stove, had not turned. She stood in the doorway for a moment, watching him. There was a curious yearning in her eyes.

By and by she said softly, "Good night, John."

He got up from his chair, and turned toward her and stood there. "Good night, Ruth," he answered.

She did not close the door between them; and after a moment, as though without his own volition, his feet moved. He came toward her, came nearer where she stood.

She did not know whether to stay or to go. The girl was shaken, unsure of herself, afraid of her own impulses. And then she remembered that she loved Darrin, must love him. And she stepped back and shut the door slowly between them. Even with the door shut she stood still, listening; and she heard John turn and go back to his chair and sit down.

She was swept by an unaccountable wave of angry disappointment. And the girl turned into her room and with quick sharp movements loosed her garments and put them aside and made herself ready for bed. She blew out the light and lay down. But her eyes were wide, and she was wholly without desire to sleep. And by and by she began to cry, for no reason she could name. She was oppressed by a terrible weight of sorrow, indefinable. It was as though this great sorrow were in the very air about her. It was, she thought once gropingly, as though someone near her were dying in the night. Once before she slept she heard Evered moving to and fro in his room, adjoining hers.

John had no heart for sleep that night. He sat in the kitchen alone for a long time; and he went to bed at last, not because he was sleepy, but because there was nothing else to do. He put wood in the stove and shut it tightly; there would be some fire there in the morning. He put the cats into the shed and locked the outer door, and so went at last to his room. The man undressed slowly and blew out his light. When once he was abed the healthy habit of his lusty youth put him quickly to sleep. He slept with scarce a dream till an hour before dawn, and woke then, and rose to dress for the morning's chores.

From his window, even before the light came, he saw that some wet snow had fallen during the night. When he had made the fire in the kitchen and filled the kettle he put on his boots and went to the barn. There were inches of snow and half-frozen mud in the barnyard. It was cold and dreary in the open. A little snow fell fitfully now and then.

Within the barn the sweet odors that he loved greeted him. The place steamed pleasantly with the body warmth of the cattle and the horse stabled there; and he heard the pigs squealing softly, as though in their sleep, in their winter pen at the farther end of the barn floor. He lighted his lantern and hung it to a peg and fed the stock—a little grain to the horse, hay to the cows, some cut-up squash and a basketful of beets to the pigs. As an afterthought he gave beets to the cows as well. John worked swiftly, cleaned up the horse's stall and the tie-up where the line of cows was secured. After he was done here he fed the bull, the red bull in its strong stall; and while the creature ate he cleaned the place and put fresh bedding in upon the floor. The bull seemed undisturbed by his presence; it turned its great head now and then to look at him with steady eyes, but there was no ugliness in its movements. When he had finished his work John stroked the great creature's flank and shoulder and neck for a moment.

He said under his breath, "You're all right, old boy. You're all right. You're clever, by golly. Clever as a cow."

When Fraternity says a beast is clever it means gentle and kind rather than shrewd. The bull seemed to understand what John said; or what lay in his tone. The great head turned and pressed against him, not roughly. John stroked it a minute more, then left the stall and took a last look round to be sure he had forgotten nothing, and then went to the house. Day was coming now; there was a ghostly gray light in the farmyard. And the snow had turned, for the time, to a drizzling, sleeting sprinkle of rain.

In the kitchen he found Ruth moving about; and she gave him the milk pails and he went out to milk. There were only three cows giving milk at that time. Two would come in in December; but for the present milking was a small chore. John was not long about it, but by the time he had finished and returned to the kitchen breakfast was almost ready. Evered had not yet come from his room.

Ruth half whispered: "He was up in the night. I think he's asleep. I'm going to let him sleep a while."

John nodded. "All right," he agreed.

"He's so tired," said Ruth; and there was a gentleness in her tone which made John look at her with some surprise. She had not spoken gently of Evered for months past.

They separated the milk and gave the cats their morning ration and then they sat themselves down and breakfasted. When they were half done Ruth saw that day was fully come, and blew out the lamp upon the table between them. It left the kitchen so bleak and cheerless, however, that she lighted it again.

"I don't like a day like this," she said. "It's ugly. Everything is ugly. It makes me nervous, somehow."

She shivered a little and looked about her as though she felt some fearful thing at her very shoulder. John, more phlegmatic, watched her in some bewilderment. Ruth was not usually nervous.

They had not heard Evered stirring; and all that morning they moved on tiptoe about their work. John forebore to split wood in the shed, his usual task on stormy days, lest he waken his father. Ruth handled the dishes gently, careful not to rattle them; she swept the floor with easy strokes that made but little sound. When Evered came into the kitchen, a little before noon, she and John looked at the man with quick curiosity, not knowing what they would see.

They saw only that Evered's head was held a little higher than was his custom of late; they saw that his eyes were sober and clear and thoughtful; they marked that his voice was gentle. He had dinner with them, speaking little, then went back to his room.

Soon after dinner Darrin came to the door. Ruth asked him in, but the man would not come. John was in the barn; and Ruth, a little uneasy and afraid before this man, wished John were here.

She asked Darrin, "Were you all right, last night?"

He said he had been comfortable; that he had been able to keep dry. He had come on no definite errand.

"I just—wanted to see you," he said.

Ruth made no reply, because she did not know what to say.

Darrin asked, "Are you all all right here?"

"Why, yes," she told him.

He looked to right and left, his eyes unable to meet hers. "Is Evered all right?" he asked.

She felt the tension in his voice without understanding it. "Yes," she said uncertainly; and then: "Why?"

He tried to laugh. "Why, nothing. Where's John?"

Ruth told him John was in the barn and Darrin went out there. Ruth was left alone in the house. Once or twice during the afternoon she saw John and Darrin in the barn door. They seemed to be doing nothing, sitting in the shelter there, whittling, smoking, talking slowly.

She felt the presence of Evered in his room, a presence like a brooding sorrow. It oppressed her. She became nervous, restless, moving aimlessly to and fro, and once she went to her room for something and found herself crying. She brushed away the tears impatiently, unable to understand. But she was afraid. There was something dreadful in the very air of the house.

At noon the wind had turned colder and for a time the sleet and rain altogether ceased. The temperature was dropping; crystals of ice formed on the puddles in the barnyard, and the patches of old snow which lay here and there stiffened like hot metal hardening in a mold. Then with the abrupt and surprising effect of a stage transformation snow began to come down from the lowering, driving clouds. This was in its way a whole-hearted snowstorm, in some contrast to the miserable drizzle of the night. It was fine and wet, and hard-driven by the wind. There were times when the barn, a little way from the house, was obscured by the flying flakes; and the trees beyond were wholly hidden behind a veil of white.

Ruth went about the house making sure that the windows were snug. From a front window she saw that the storm had thinned in that direction. She was able to look down into the orchard, which lay a little below the house, sloping away toward North Fraternity. The nearer trees were plain, the others were hidden from sight.

The driving wind plastered this wet snow against everything it touched. One side of every tree, one side of every twig assumed a garment of white. The windows which the wind struck were opaque with it. When Ruth went back to the kitchen she saw that a whole side of the barn was so completely covered by the snow blanket that the dark shingling was altogether hidden. Against the white background of the storm it was as though this side of the barn had ceased to exist. The illusion was so abrupt that for a moment it startled her.

The snow continued to fall for much of the afternoon; then the storm drifted past them and the hills all about were lighted up, not by the sun itself, but by an eerie blue light, which may have been the sun refracted and reflected by the snow that was still in the air above. The storm had left a snowy covering upon the world; and even this white blanket had a bluish tinge. Snow clung to windward of every tree and rock and building. Even the clothesline in the yard beside the house was hung with it.

At first, when the storm had but just passed, the scene was very beautiful; but in the blue light it was pitilessly, bleakly cold. Then distantly the sun appeared. Ruth saw it first indirectly. Down the valley to the southward, a valley like a groove between two hills, the low scurrying clouds began to lift; and so presently the end of the valley was revealed, and Ruth was able to look through beneath the screen of clouds, and she could see the slopes of a distant hill where the snow had fallen lightly, brilliantly illumined by the golden sun—gold on the white of the snow and the brown and the green of grass and of trees. Mystically beautiful—blue sky in the distance there; and, between, the sun-dappled hills. The scene was made more gorgeous by the somber light which still lay about the farm.

Then the clouds lifted farther and the sun came nearer. A little before sunset blue skies showed overhead, the sun streamed across the farm, the snow that had stuck against everything it touched began to sag and drop away; and the dripping of melting snow sounded cheerfully in the stillness of the late afternoon.

Ruth saw John and Darrin in the farmyard talking together, watching the skies. They came toward the house and John bade her come out to see. The three of them walked round to the front, where the eye might reach for miles into infinite vistas of beauty. They stood there for a little time.

The dropping sun bathed all the land in splendor; the winds had passed, the air was still as honey. Earth was become a thing of glory beyond compare.

They were still standing here when they heard the hoarse and furious bellow of the great red bull.

# CHAPTER XVIII

EVERED had not slept the night before. There was no sleep in the man. And this was not because he was torn and agonized; it was because he had never been so fully alive, so alert of mind and body.

Darrin's accusation had come to him as no shock; Darrin's proof that his wife was loyal had come as no surprise. He had expected neither; yet when they came it seemed to the man that he must have known they would come. It seemed to him that all the world must know what he had done; and it seemed to him that he must always have known his wife was—his wife forever.

His principal reaction was a great relief of spirit. He was unhappy, sorrowful; yet there was a pleasant ease and solace in his very unhappiness. For he was rid now, at last, of doubts and of uncertainties; his mind was no more beclouded; there were no more shadows of mystery and questioning. All was clear before him; all that there was to know he knew. And—his secret need no longer be borne alone. Darrin knew; it was as though the whole world knew. He was indescribably relieved by this certainty.

He did not at first look into the future at all. He let himself breathe the present. He came back to the farm and ate his supper and went to his room; and there was something that sang softly within him. It was almost as though his wife waited for him, comfortingly, there. Physically a little restless, he moved about for a time; but his mind was steady, his thoughts were calm.

His thoughts were memories, harking backward through the years.

Evered was at this time almost fifty years old. He was born in North Fraternity, in the house of his mother's father, to which she had gone when her time came near. Evered's own father had died weeks before, in the quiet fashion of the countryside. That had been on this hillside farm above the swamp, which Evered's father had owned. His mother stayed upon the farm for a little, and when the time came she went to her home, and when Evered was a month old she had brought him back to the farm again.

She died, Evered remembered, when he was still a boy, nine or ten years old. She had not married a second time, but her brother had come to live with her, and he survived her and kept the farm alive and producing. He taught Evered the work that lay before him. He had been a butcher, and it was from him Evered learned the trade. A kind man, Evered remembered, but not over wise; and he had lacked understanding of the boy.

Evered had been a brilliant boy, active and wholly alive, his mind alert and keen, his muscles quick, his temper sharp. Yet his anger was accustomed to pass quickly, so that he had in him the stuff that makes friends; and he had friends in those days. Still in his teens he won the friendship of the older men, even as he dominated the boys of his own age. He and Lee Motley had grown up together. There had always been close sympathy between these two.

When he was nineteen he married, in the adventurous spirit of youth, a girl of the hills; a simple lovely child, not so old as he. Married her gaily, brought her home gaily. There had been affection between them, he knew now, but nothing more. He had thought himself heartbroken when, their boy child still a baby, she had died. But a year later he met Mary MacLure, and there had never been any other woman in the world for him thereafter.

Evered's memories were very vivid; it needed no effort to bring back to him Mary's face as he first saw her. A dance in the big hall halfway from North Fraternity to Montville. She came late, two men with her; and Evered saw her come into the door. He had come alone to the dance; he was free to devote himself to her, and within the half hour he had swept all others aside, and he and Mary MacLure danced and danced together, while their pulses sang in the soft air of the night, and their eyes, meeting, glowed and glowed.

Fraternity still talked of that swift, hot courtship. Evered had fought two men for her, and that fight was well remembered. He had fought for a clear field, and won it, though Mary MacLure scolded him for the winning, as long as she had heart to scold this man. From his first moment with her Evered had been lifted out of himself by the emotions she awoke in him. He loved her hotly and jealously and passionately; and in due course he won her.

Not too quickly, for Mary MacLure knew her worth and knew how to make herself dear to him. She humbled him, and at first he suffered this, till one night he came to her house when the flowers were abloom and the air was warm as a caress. And at first, seated on the steps of her porch with the man at her feet, she teased him lightly and provokingly, till he rose and stood above her. Something made her rise too; and then she was in his arms, lips yielding to his, trembling to his ardent whispers. For long minutes they stood so, conscious only of each other, drunk with the mutual ecstasy of conquest and of surrender, tempestuously embracing.

They were married, and he brought her home to the farm above the swamp, and because he loved her so well, because he loved her too well, he had watched over her with jealous eyes, had guarded her. She became a recluse. An isolation grew up about them. Evered wanted no human being in his life but her; and when the ardor of his love could find no other vent, it showed itself in cruel gibes at her, in reckless words.

Youth was still hot in the man. He and Mary might have weathered this hard period of adjustment, might have come to a quiet happiness together;

but it was in these years that Evered killed Dave Riggs, a thing half accident. He had gone forth that day with bitterness in his heart; he had quarreled with Mary, and hated himself for it; and hated by proxy all the world besides. Riggs irritated him profoundly, roused the quick anger in the man. And when the hot clouds cleared from before his eyes Riggs was dead.

A thing that could not be undone, it had molded Evered's soul into harsh and rugged lines. It was true, as he had told Darrin, that he had sought to make some amends; had offered help to the dead man's wife, first openly, and then—when she cursed him from her door—in secret, hidden ways. But she left Fraternity and took her child, and they lost themselves in the outer world.

So Evered could not ease his conscience by the reparation he longed to make; and the thing lay with him always through the years thereafter. A thing fit to change a man in unpleasant fashion, the killing had shaped Evered's whole life—to this black end that lay before him.

The man during this long night alone in his room thought back through all the years; and it was as though he sat in judgment on himself. There was, there had always been a native justice in him; he never deceived his own heart, never palliated even to himself his own ill deeds. There was no question in his mind now. He knew the thing he had done in all its ugly lights. And as he thought of it, sitting beside his bed, he played with the heavy knife which he had carried all these years. He fondled the thing in his hand, eyes half closed as he stared at it. He was not conscious that he held it. Yet it had become almost a part of him through long habit; and it was as much a part of him now as his own hand that held it. The heavy haft balanced so familiarly.

The night, and then the day. A steady calm possessed him. His memories flowed smoothly past, like the eternal cycle of the days. The man's face did not change; he was expressionless. He was sunk so deep in his own thoughts that the turmoil there did not disturb his outward aspect. His countenance was grave and still. No tears flowed; this was no time for tears. It was an hour too deep for tears, a sorrow beyond weeping.

During the storm that day he went to the window now and then. And once in the morning he heard the red bull bellow in its pen; and once or twice thereafter, as the afternoon drove slowly on. Each time he heard this sound it was as though the man's attention was caught and held. He stood still in a listening attitude, as though waiting for the bellow to be repeated; and it would be minutes on end before his eyes clouded with his own thoughts again.

It would be easy to say that Evered during this solitary night and day went mad with grief and self-condemning, but it would not be true. The man was never more sane. His thoughts were profound, but they were quiet and slow and unperturbed. They were almost impersonal. There is in most men—though in few women—this power to withdraw out of oneself or into an inner deeper self; this power to stand as spectator of one's own actions. It is a manifestation of a deeper, more remote consciousness. It is as though there were a man within a man. And this inner soul has no emotions. It is unmoved by love or passion, by anger or hatred, by sorrow or grief, by hunger or by thirst. It watches warm caresses, it hears ardent words, it sees fierce blows, and listens to curses and lamentations with the same inscrutable and immutable calm. It can approve, it can condemn; but it neither rejoices nor bemoans. It is always conscious that the moment is nothing, eternity everything; that the whole alone has portent and importance. This inner self has a depth beyond plumbing; it has a strength unshakable; it has understanding beyond belief. It is not conscience, for it sets itself up as no arbiter of acts or deeds. It is simply a consciousness that that which is done is good or evil, kind or harsh, wise or foolish. This calm inner soul of souls might be called God in man.

Evered this day lived in this inner consciousness. As though he sat remote above the stream he watched the years of his memories flow by. He was, after the first moments, torn by no racking grief and wrenched by no remorseful torments and burned by no agonizing fires. He was without emotion, but not without judgment and not without decision. He moved through his thoughts as though to a definitely appointed and pre-determined end. A strange numbness possessed him, in which only his mind was alive.

He did not pity himself; neither did he damn himself. He did not pray that he might cancel all the past, for this inner consciousness knew the past could never be canceled. He simply thought upon it, with grave and sober consideration.

When his thoughts evidenced themselves in actions it was done slowly, and as though he did know not what he did. He got up from where he had been sitting and went to the window and looked out. The snow had ceased; the sun was breaking through. The world was never more beautiful, never more gloriously white and clean.

The man had held in his hands for most of the day that heavy knife of his. He put it now back in its sheath. Then he took off his shirt and washed himself. There was no fire of purpose in his eye; he was utterly calm and unhurried.

He put on a clean shirt. It was checked blue and white. Mary Evered had made it for him, as she was accustomed to make most of his clothes.

When it was buttoned he drew his belt about him and buckled it snug. Then he sat down and took off his slippers—old, faded, rundown things that had eased his tired feet night by night for years. He took off these slippers and put on hobnailed shoes, lacing them securely.

When this was done the man stood for a little in the room, and he looked steadily before him. His eyes did not move to this side and that; there was no suggestion that he was taking farewell of the familiar things about him. It was more as though he looked upon something which other eyes could never see. And his face lighted a little; it was near smiling. There was peace in it.

I do not believe that there was any deadly purpose in Evered's heart when he left his room. Fraternity thinks so; Fraternity has never thought anything else about the matter. He took his knife, in its sheath. That is proof enough for Fraternity. "He went to do the bull, and the bull done him." That is what they say, have always said.

It does not occur to them that the man took the knife because he was a man; because it was not in him to lay down his life supinely; because battle had always been in his blood and was his instinct. It does not occur to them that there was in Evered's mind this day the purpose of atonement, and nothing more. For Fraternity had never plumbed the man, had never understood him.

No matter. No need to dig for hidden things. Enough to know what Evered did.

He went from his room into the kitchen. No one was there. Ruth and John and Darrin were outside in front of the house. Thus they did not see him come out into the barnyard and go steadily and surely across and past the corner of the barn, till he came to the high-boarded walls of the red bull's pen.

He put his hand against these board walls for a moment, with a gesture not unlike that of a blind man. One watching would have supposed that he walked unseeingly or that his eyes were closed. He went along the wall of the pen until he came to the narrow gate, set between two of the cedar posts, through which it was possible to enter.

Evered opened this gate, stepped inside the pen and shut the gate behind him. He took half a dozen paces forward, into the center of the inclosure, and stood still.

The red bull had heard the gate open; and the creature turned in its stall and came to the door between stall and pen. It saw Evered standing there; and after a moment the beast came slowly out, moving one foot at a time, carefully, like a watchful antagonist—came out till it was clear of the stall; till it and the man faced each other, not twenty feet apart.

After a moment the bull lowered its great head and emitted a harsh and angry bellow that was like a roar.

# CHAPTER XIX

THE beauty of the whole world in this hour should be remembered. Houses, trees, walls, shrubs, knolls—all were overlaid with the snow blanket inches deep. It had been faintly blue, this carpet of snow, in the first moments after the storm passed, and before the sun had broken through. When the sun illumined the hill about the farm the snow was dazzling white, blinding the eye with a thousand gleams, as though it were diamond dust spread all about them. Afterward, when John and Darrin and Ruth had passed to the front of the house to look across the valley and away, the sun descending lost its white glare; its rays took on a crimson hue. Where they struck the snow fairly it was rose pink; where shadows lay the blue was coming back again. The air was so clear that it seemed not to exist, yet did exist as a living, pulsing color which was all about—faint, hardly to be seen.

The three stood silent, watching all this. Ruth could not have spoken if she had wished to do so; she could scarce breathe. Darrin watched unseeingly, automatically, his thoughts busy elsewhere. John stood still, and his eyes were narrowed and his face was faintly flushed, either by the sun's light or by the intoxication of beauty which was spread before him. And they were standing thus when there came to them through the still, liquid air the bellow of the bull.

John and Ruth reacted automatically to that sound. They were accustomed to the beast; they could to some extent distinguish between its outcries, guess at its moods from them. Its roaring was always frightful to an unaccustomed ear; but they were used to it, were disturbed only by some foreign note in the sound. They both knew now that the bull was murderously angry. They did not know, had no way of knowing what had roused it. It might be a dog, a cat; it might be that one of the cows had broken loose and was near its stall; it might be a pig; it might be a hen; it might be merely a rat running in awkward loping bounds across its pen. They did not stop to wonder; but John turned and ran toward the pen, and Ruth followed him, stumbling through the soft snow. Darrin, to whom the bull's bellow had always been a frightful sound, was startled by it, would have asked a question. When he saw them run round the house he followed them.

John was in the lead, but Ruth was swift footed and was at his shoulder when he reached the gate of the pen. The walls of the inclosure and the gate itself were so high that they could not look over the top. But just beside the main gate there was a smaller one, like a door; too narrow and too low for the bull to pass, but large enough for a man. John fumbled with the latch of this gate; and his moment's delay gave the others time to come up with him. When he opened the way and stepped into the pen Ruth and Darrin were at his shoulder. Thus that which was in the pen broke upon them all three at once—a picture never to be forgotten, indelibly imprinted on their minds.

The snow that had fallen in the inclosure was trampled here and there by the tracks of the bull and by the tracks of the man, and in one spot it was torn and tossed and crushed into mud, as though the two had come together there in some strange matching of strength. At this spot too there was a dark patch upon the snow; a patch that looked almost black. Yet Ruth knew what had made this patch, and clutched at her throat to stifle her scream; and John knew, and Darrin knew. And the two men were sick and shaken.

At the other side of the pen, perhaps a dozen long paces from where they stood, Evered and the bull faced each other. Neither had heard their coming, neither had seen them. They were, for the fraction of a second, motionless. The great bull's head was lowered; its red neck was streaked with darker red where a long gash lay. From this gash dripped and dripped and spurted a little stream, a dark and ugly stream.

The man, Evered, stood erect and still, facing the bull. They saw that he bore the knife in his left hand; and they saw that his right arm was helpless, hanging in a curiously twisted way, bent backward below the elbow. The sleeve of his checked shirt was stained there, and his hand was red. His shoulder seemed somehow distorted. Yet he was erect and strong, and his face was steady and curiously peaceful, and he made no move to escape or to flee.

An eternity that was much less than a second passed while no man moved, while the bull stood still. Then its short legs seemed to bend under it; its great body hurtled forward. The vast bulk moved quick as light. It was upon the man.

They saw Evered strike, lightly, with his left hand; and there was no purpose behind the blow. It had not the strength to drive it home. At the same time the man leaped to one side, sliding his blade down the bull's shoulder; leaped lightly and surely to one side. The bull swept almost past the man, the great head showed beyond him.

Then the head swung back and struck Evered in the side, and he fell, over and over, rolling like a rabbit taken in midleap by the gunner's charge of shot. And the red bull turned as a hound might have turned, with a speed that was unbelievable. Its head, its forequarters rose; they saw its feet come down with a curious chopping stroke—apparently not so desperately hard—saw its feet come down once, and twice upon the prostrate man.

It must be remembered that all this had passed quickly. It was no more than a fifth of a second that John Evered stopped within the gate of the pen. Then he was leaping toward the bull, and Ruth followed him. Darrin crouched in the gate, and his face was white as death. He cried, "Come back, Ruth!" And even as she ran after John she had time to look back toward Darrin and see him cowering there.

John took off his coat as he ran, took it off with a quick whipping motion. He swung it back behind him, round his head. And then as the bull's body rose for another deadly downward hoofstroke John struck it in the flank with all his weight. He caught the beast faintly off balance, so that the bull pivoted on its hind feet, away from the fallen man; and before the great creature could turn John whipped his coat into its face, lashing it again and again. The bull shook its great head, turning away from the blinding blows; and John caught the coat about its head and held it there, his arms fairly round the bull's neck. He was shouting, shouting into its very ear. Ruth even in that moment heard him. And she marked that his tone was gentle, quieting, kind. There was no harshness in it.

She needed no telling what to do. John had swung the bull away from Evered; he had the creature blinded. She bent beside the prostrate man and tried to drag him to his feet, but Evered bent weakly in the middle. He was conscious, he looked up at her, his face quite calm and happy; and he shook his head. He said, "Go."

The girl caught him beneath the shoulders and tried to drag him backward through the soft snow across the pen. It was hard work. John still blinding the bull, still calling out to the beast, was working it away from her.

She could not call on him for help; she turned and cried to Darrin, "Help me—carry him."

Darrin came cautiously into the pen and approached her and took her arm. "Come away," he said.

Her eyes blazed at him; and she cried again, "Carry him out."

He said huskily, "Leave him. Leave him here. Come away."

She had never released Evered's shoulders, never ceased to tug at him. But Darrin took her arm now as though to pull her away; and she swung toward him so fiercely that he fell back from her. The girl began abruptly to cry; half with anger at Darrin, half with pity for the broken man in her arms. And she tugged and tugged, sliding the limp body inch by inch toward safety.

Then she saw John beside her. He had guided the bull, half forcing, half persuading, to the entrance into the stall; he had worked the creature in, prodding it, urging; and shut and made secure the door. Now he was at her side. He knelt with her.

"He's terribly hurt," she said through her tears.

John nodded. "I'll take him," he told her.

So he gathered Evered into his arms, gathered him up so tenderly, and held the man against his breast, and Ruth supported Evered's drooping head as she walked beside John. They came to the gate and it was too narrow for them to pass through. So Ruth went through alone, to open the wider gate from the outside.

She found Darrin there, standing uncertainly. She looked at him as she might have looked at a stranger. She was hardly conscious that he was there at all. When he saw what she meant to do he would have helped her. She turned to him then, and she seemed to bring her thoughts back from a great distance; she looked at him for a moment and then she said, "Go away!"

He cried, "Ruth! Please——"

She repeated, "I want you to go away. Oh," she cried, "go away! Don't ever come here again!"

Darrin moved back a step, and she swung the gate open so that John could come through, and closed it behind him, and walked with him to the kitchen door, supporting Evered's head. Darrin hesitated, then followed them uncertainly.

When they came to the door Ruth opened it, and John—moving sidewise so that his burden should not brush against the door frame—went into the kitchen, and across. Ruth passed round him to open the door into Evered's own room; and John went through.

When he reached the bedside and turned to lay Evered there he missed Ruth. He looked toward the kitchen; and he saw her standing in the outer doorway. Darrin was on the steps before her. John heard Darrin say something pleadingly. Ruth stood still for a moment. Then John saw her slowly shut the door, shutting out the other man. And he saw her turn the key and shoot the bolt.

She came toward him, running; and her eyes were full of tears.

They laid Evered on his own bed, the bed he and Mary Evered had shared. Ruth put the pillow under his head; and because it was cold in the room she would have drawn a blanket across him. John shook his head. He was loosening the other's garments, making swift examination of his father's hurts, pressing and probing firmly here and there.

Evered had drifted out of consciousness on the way to the house; but his eyes opened now and there was sweat on his forehead. He looked up at them steadily and soberly enough.

"You hurt me, John," he said.

Ruth whispered, "I'll telephone the doctor."

Evered turned his head a little on the pillow, and looked toward her. "No," he said, "no need."

"Oh, there must be!" she cried. "There must be! He can——"

Evered interrupted her. "Don't go, Ruthie. I want to talk to you."

She was crying; she came slowly back to the bedside. The sun was ready to dip behind the hills. Its last rays coming through the window fell across her face. She was somehow glorified. She put her hand on Evered's head, and he—the native strength still alive within him—reached up and caught it in his and held it firmly thereafter for a space.

"You're crying," he said.

"I can't help it," she told him.

"Why are you crying?" he asked.

"Because I'm so sorry for you."

A slow wave of happiness crept into his eyes. "You're a good girl, Ruthie. You mustn't cry for me."

She brushed her sleeve across her eyes. "Why did you do it?" she asked almost fiercely. "Why did you let him get at you?"

"You've been hating me, Ruthie," he told her gently. "Why do you cry for me?"

"Oh," she told him, "I don't hate you now. I don't hate you now."

He said weakly, "You've reason to hate me."

"No, no!" she said. "Don't be unhappy. You never meant—you loved Mary."

"Aye," he agreed, "I loved Mary. I loved Mary, and John loves you."

She was sitting on the edge of the bed, John standing beside her; but she did not look up at him. Her eyes were all for Evered.

"Please," she said. "Rest. Let me get the doctor."

His head moved slowly in negation. "Something to tell you, Ruth, first—before the doctor comes."

She looked toward John then, for decision or for reassurance. His eyes answered her; they bade her listen; they told her there was no work for the doctor here. So she turned back to Evered again. He was speaking slowly; she caught his words bending above him.

It was thus that the man told the story at last, without heat or passion, neither sparing himself nor condemning himself, but as though he spoke of another man. And he spoke of little things that he had not been conscious of noticing at the time—how when he took down his revolver to go after the bull the cats were frightened and ran from him; how as he passed through the barnyard the horse whinnied from its stall; how he was near stumbling over a ground sparrow's nest in the open land above the woodlot; how a red squirrel mocked at him from a hemlock as he went on his way. It was as though he lived the day over while they listened. He told how he had come out above the spring; how he saw Mary and Dane Semler there.

"I believed she loved him," he said.

And Ruth cried, "Oh, she never loved anyone but you." She was not condemning, she was reassuring him; and he understood, his hand tightening on hers.

"I know," he said. "And my unbelief was my great wrong to Mary; worse than the other."

He went on steadily enough. "There was time," he told her. "I could have turned him, stopped him, shot him. But I hated her; I let the bull come on."

The girl scarce heard him. His words meant little to her; her sympathy for him was so profound that her only concern was to ease the man and make him happier.

She cried, "Don't, don't torment yourself! Please, I understand."

"I killed her," he said.

And as one would soothe a child, while the tears ran down her cheeks she bade him never mind.

"There, there. Never mind," she pleaded.

"I killed her, but I loved her," he went on implacably.

And he told them something of his sorrow afterward, and told them how he had stifled his remorse by telling himself that Mary was false; how he had kept his soul alive with that poor unction. He was weakening fast; the terrific battering which he had endured was having its effect upon even his great strength; but his voice went steadily on.

He came to Darrin, came to that scene with Darrin the night before, by the spring; and so told how Darrin had proved to him that Mary was— Mary. And at last, as though they must understand, he added, "So then I knew."

They did not ask what he knew; these two did understand. They knew the man as no others would ever know him—knew his heart, knew his unhappiness. There was no need of his telling them how he had passed the night, and then the day. He did not try.

Ruth was comforting him; and he watched her with a strange and wistful light in his eyes.

"You've hated me, Ruthie," he reminded her. "Do you hate me now?"

There was no hate in her, nothing but a flooding sympathy and sorrow for the broken man. She cried, "No, no!"

"You're forgiving——"

"Yes. Please—please know."

"Then Mary will," he murmured half to himself.

Ruth nodded, and told him, "Yes, yes; she will. Please, never fear."

For a little while he was silent, while she spoke to him hungrily and tenderly, as a mother might have spoken; and her arms round him seemed to feel the man slipping away. She was weeping terribly; and he put up one hand and brushed her eyes.

"Don't cry," he bade her. "It's all right, don't cry."

"I can't help it. I don't want to help it. Oh, if there was only anything I could do."

He smiled faintly; and his words were so husky she could scarcely hear.

"Go to John," he said.

She held him closer. "Please——"

"Please go to John," he urged again.

She still held him, but her arms relaxed a little. She looked up at John, and saw the young man standing there beside her. And a picture came back to her—the picture of John throwing himself against the red bull's flank, blinding it, urging it away. His voice had been so gentle, and sure, and strong. She herself in that moment had burned with hate of the bull. Yet there had been no hate in John, nothing but gentleness and strength.

She had coupled him with Evered in her thoughts for so long that there was a strange illumination in her memories now; she saw John as though she had never seen him before; and almost without knowing it she rose and stood before him.

John made no move to take her; but she put her arms round his neck and drew his head down. Only then did his arms go about her and hold her close. There was infinite comfort in them. He bent and kissed her. And strangely she thought of Darrin. There had been something hard and cruel in his embrace, there had been loneliness in his arms. There was only gentleness in John's; and she was not lonely here. She looked up, smiling through her tears.

"Oh, John, John!" she whispered.

As they kissed so closely, the warm light from the west came through the window and enfolded them. And Evered, upon the bed, wearily turned his head till he could see them, watch them. While he watched, his eyes lighted with a slow contentment. And after a little a smile crept across his face, such a smile as comes only with supreme happiness and peace. A kindly, loving smile.

He was still smiling when they turned toward him again; but they understood at once that Evered himself had gone away.

THE END.

Milton Keynes UK
Ingram Content Group UK Ltd.
UKHW040900050124
435493UK00006B/981